The Gravemen

The Gravemen
By Melissa North

Published by Less Than Three Press LLC

Edited by J. Ang
Cover designed by Aisha Akeju

Print Edition May 2013
Copyright © 2013 by Melissa North
First Edition Copyright © Melissa North October 2011
Printed in the United States of America

ISBN 9781620042076

The Gravemen

Melissa North

Chapter One

Asdelar Lorem had himself a lap full of giggling simpering prostitute.

Again.

Hinego studied his companion's rather foolish smile from across the room for a moment before disgust won over tact. Muttering under his breath, he strode across the tavern floor. Those few who were in his way hastily cleared a path. Hinego was not overly tall for a man, nor was he particularly bulky, but the red sash across his chest and back was as effective as a drawn weapon. It labeled him as one of the Imalt-wor, the fearsome law keepers of the crown and noblemen, and anyone with half a brain knew better than to make himself a visible target when such a man had an expression like a thundercloud marring his otherwise handsome features.

He stopped beside Asdelar's table and offered the whore a look that could have curdled milk. She gaped at him for a moment, then scrambled to her feet and hastened off a trifle huffily.

Asdelar watched her go, bewildered, before turning. He winced as he, too, got caught in the blast of Hinego's glare. "Something I can help you with, Idra?" he asked innocently.

Hinego seated himself across from Asdelar, dark

eyes hard. "What do you think you're doing?"

"What, her?" Asdelar leaned over slightly to catch another glimpse of the woman, looking put-out when he spotted her already flattering her next potential customer by the hearth. "Just a bit of fun. Loosen up."

"Loosen up?" Hinego stared at him incredulously. He put his fists in his lap before he could be tempted to use them and leaned across the table to hiss, "You do not have the time or luxury for such disgusting deviations, Blade. And I have not the patience for it. Your King entrusted you with a task, and here you are trying to get inside the skirt of every whore and painted boy in the town limits."

Looking unimpressed by what Hinego personally thought was a remarkable control of temper, Asdelar flapped a hand carelessly, reaching for his tankard. "You don't need to preach duty to me, Idra. I'm well aware of what's expected of me." He sighed into his drink, voice just this side of sulky. "Can you really blame me for trying to find a bit of fun on such a dismal trip? Honestly, I can't understand how His Majesty can dote on the monstrous little brat so. He's probably fonder of her than her own father."

Hinego's mouth dropped open. He shot a quick look around to make sure their conversation wasn't being overheard, speaking quietly but sharply. "You forget yourself, Blade. Lady Valera is—"

"A spoiled, snobbish brat," Asdelar finished firmly, setting his tankard aside with a look of distaste. "And everyone in the kingdom knows it—including her father the Duke. She's always pulling stunts like this: running away just to make her parents worry. Never this long, maybe, but I still think the King's overreacting by sending Gravemen after her. And I thought I asked you to stop calling me 'Blade' all the time. I have a name, you know."

"Your personal opinion of the Duke's daughter is irrelevant," he snapped, ignoring that last part. "We have a job to do, and I don't have the time to go searching every brothel for you. And if you contract a disease, so help me, I'll leave you to rot in the bed I find you in."

Though his expression was wounded, there was a hint of amusement in Asdelar's blue eyes. "I knew Reds were reputed to be cruel, but I don't think I've ever met one so upfront about it as you, Idra."

Hinego straightened in his chair, looking down his nose at Asdelar in thinly veiled contempt. "You represent the whole of the Banam-hin, Lorem. It's rare for civilians see your kind outside the palace walls, and they'll be watching you with some curiosity. I'm beginning to wonder if that means anything to you."

"Oh, come off it." Asdelar propped his chin in his hand and grinned at him insultingly. "No one's going to know I'm a Blade just by looking at me." He directed his pointed gaze towards Hinego's red sash. "You're the one who stands out like a sore thumb, my friend."

He knew Asdelar was just trying to get a rise out of him; Asdelar seemed to find a sick amusement in baiting him since they'd met. But he couldn't bite back a retort. "Commoners aren't allowed to carry weapons, imbecile. That sword at your hip is enough of a hint."

Asdelar waved off his words carelessly. "They'll think I'm an ordinary soldier or nobleman's messenger. Without my armor I'm just another rich man's errand boy for all they know."

He gritted his teeth, but couldn't think of a satisfactory argument to that. As much as it pained him to admit it, the fool had a point. The Banam-hin were most distinguishable by the intricate engravings on their armor, but any man of higher class was permitted to carry a sword for self-protection. With his armor prudently dismantled and stashed in their saddlebags, there was nothing to positively identify Asdelar as the elite swordsman he truly was. His weapon, airs and well-groomed looks could easily be dismissed as natural in some Duke's flighty son or nephew.

Hinego, however, had not bothered to disguise himself. He packed only the simplest of his clothing, for the more flowing traditional garb he was accustomed to would only be ruined by such a trip. But he refused to remove the red sash that identified him as a member of King Dyggha's other elite force, the Imalt-wor or "Reds". Both forces fell under the more grim title of the King's Gravemen, as they were known to be the strongest and deadliest of his troops, though each branch had distinctly different duties and techniques. The Reds were specifically intended to be shuffled about the country, keeping the discipline firm in towns and acting as temporary law enforcement for whichever Duchy their King lent them out to. They were soldiers for the country at large, and accustomed to getting the respect and obedience of the people throughout the country with their mere presence.

In contrast, the Blades were purely a home guard, unused to life outside the palace or the city on its doorstep. Originally bred for war, they were in truth more for show in current times of peace. A Blade outside the palace walls would earn them a bit more attention than they currently needed, and so it was Hinego who used his influence and authority to speed up their trip.

Asdelar, on the other hand, seemed to be enjoying his new-found anonymity a bit too much.

"This is not a vacation, Lorem," Hinego said firmly. "We find the King's great-niece and we haul her back home. We don't have time for distractions. No more prostitutes, end of discussion."

A hint of annoyance finally flickered across Asdelar's face. "No one but the King tells a Blade what to do, Idra," he said with a note of steel in his voice. "We'll find the little monster. But there's no harm in having some fun along the way."

"There's plenty of harm," Hinego said hotly, but Asdelar rose to his feet just then as if bored of the conversation. Hinego was too startled by the insult at first to be angry. "Where are you going?"

"We've an early start tomorrow," Asdelar reminded him with a small shrug. "Since you've managed to scare off any entertainment for the night I might have otherwise enjoyed, I'm off to bed. Though if I hear sounds through the wall that indicate you've taken her to your own bed, I admit I'll be quite peevish with you tomorrow. Good night!"

"Why you—I would never—" Hinego was left sputtering in indignant horror; Asdelar was already heading up the stairs. Fuming, he snatched up the discarded tankard and took a quick gulp in an attempt to cool his temper.

It tasted like ditch water. Putting it aside in

disgust, Hinego rose from the table. Asdelar was right in one respect: they had an early start in the morning. And their quarry's trail grew colder every day.

~~*

They were on the road again shortly after sunrise, much to Asdelar's displeasure. He yawned loudly and frequently, but his unspoken protests were steadfastly ignored.

"Still no word," Hinego said, turning his horse to the left when they reached a fork in the road. "We've been to three different villages in the past week, and no one has seen so much as a freckle of the Duke's daughter. It's obvious she didn't come this way. We'll try south instead."

Asdelar twisted in his saddle, looking around at the plain countryside. "Are you sure? There are still more villages we can try—"

"We agreed that I would be the one to set the pace and choose the route, Lorem," Hinego interrupted curtly. "The Reds are accustomed to traveling the roads and are familiar with the land, while you home guard never set foot outside of your precious city."

Asdelar bristled a bit at that, frowning. "This habit you have of referring to the Banam-hin as the King's lapdogs is growing tiresome," he said.

Face expressionless, Hinego didn't even spare him a glance. "I never put it in those exact words," he pointed out. "Although I see no reason to dismiss that description."

Asdelar's eyes narrowed. "Just because the

Blades' sole loyalty is to their King does not give you or any man the right to treat us with such disrespect."

"Please." Hinego's mouth curled in an artful sneer. "Do you think I don't know what you people say behind the Reds' backs? I believe you refer to us as ... 'weaponless mercenaries', wasn't it?"

Glancing away, Asdelar coughed. "Not every Blade speaks of the Reds in that way."

"I'm sure." Hinego's voice dripped sarcasm. "You Blades are so full of your own self-importance it's sickening. And you seem to think that no man is complete without a weapon at his side."

"Stop putting words in my mouth," Asdelar protested. "I've never said anything like that. Everyone knows the Reds are perfectly capable without weapons."

Hinego snorted, but didn't respond, and they spent the next several hours in tense silence.

By the time they finally stopped at the side of the road to stretch their legs and have a quick lunch, Asdelar seemed to have forgotten about their earlier argument. He ate quickly and lay in the grass, hands tucked under his head as he watched the clouds move by. This far from the city there were more stretches of uninterrupted plains than he'd ever seen before. The grass roots were too tough for farming, leaving open grasslands in every direction for miles. They hadn't even passed another traveler in hours. It gave the impression that Asdelar and Hinego were the only two left in the world.

Seating himself several yards away, Hinego ignored Asdelar completely as he ate his own bread and cheese, attention on the short message he was composing. He checked it over once he was finished, rolled it up tightly, then rose to his feet. He pressed his tongue against his teeth, giving a shrill whistle.

Asdelar turned his head to watch in interest. "Why bother to send a message? We haven't had any luck, and His Majesty won't be happy that this is the second correspondence outlining our failure."

Hinego folded back one sleeve, revealing the thick leather gauntlet that reached nearly to his elbow. "He expects us to keep him up to date," he said curtly. "It doesn't matter whether we've found any hint of the Lady or not."

Asdelar rolled his eyes. "And you call us the lapdogs," he muttered. "You know, you'd be a lot more attractive if you weren't so contrary."

He glared at Asdelar mutely. For the hundredth time he found himself cursing his ill luck. Being paired up with a Blade for the mission was bad enough. But of all the Banam-hin, it was Asdelar who'd been nominated by his Captain. The two of them had been bickering since day one.

Like many Reds, Hinego was confident and arrogant almost to a fault. His boyish attitude and unscrupulous habits offended Hinego. Still, things might have been a bit less tense between them if he didn't have such a lightning-quick temper.

Hinego was slim and wiry and stood at a fairly unintimidating height of five-ten. He was darkly tanned as all the Reds were from years of traveling the roads, and his eyes were even blacker than his windswept hair.

Asdelar, of course, was Hinego's complete opposite in both looks and manner. Tall, broad-shouldered, with blue eyes and perfectly-combed blond hair, Asdelar looked more like a pampered aristocrat than a warrior. He liked the sound of his own voice and demonstrated this by cheerfully filling in the silence during their journey with colorful jokes and stories that fell on uncaring ears. He was quite handsome and seemed to have no problem using his charm and looks to his own advantage, much to Hinego's disgust.

Asdelar had very quickly figured out just how touchy Hinego was about certain things, and seemed to find perverse pleasure in constantly teasing and baiting him to get a reaction. He'd learned quickly that the occasional flirtatious remark always seemed to work best.

Hinego had seriously contemplated the idea of gutting Asdelar with his own sword on more than one occasion.

There was a screech from above, and a small, rust-colored hawk dove from the sky, flaring its wings at the last instant to slow its descent. It landed on Hinego's outstretched arm, vicious talons clinging to the protective leather, and cocked its head to stare at Asdelar with one fierce yellow eye.

Asdelar stared back warily, remaining perfectly still on his spot in the grass. "That thing looks like it could tear out a man's eyes," he noted. "I can't believe you let it get so close to you."

Hinego stroked the bird's head briefly with a fingertip before sliding the rolled message into the tiny canister attached firmly to the hawk's foot. "Messenger hawks are quite common among the Imalt-wor. It's necessary when you travel as much as we do." He lowered his arm, then jerked it up quickly. The hawk sprang from her perch, wings flapping. Within moments she was nothing, but a dot in the sky. Hinego watched her go with an unreadable expression on his face, hand lifted to shield his eyes from the sun. "I raised Dora from a chick. She would never harm me intentionally."

It was the first personal thing he'd let slip. Asdelar sat up, choosing his words carefully to avoid alienating him again. "She's tame, then?"

"Of course she's not." Hinego sent him a brief look as if to say 'Don't be stupid'. "She's a hawk, not a dog. She wouldn't react well to anyone else attempting to touch her, so I suggest you keep your hands to yourself when she's around and don't make any sudden movements." He stopped suddenly and frowned. Turning away, he headed for his horse, tugging his sleeve back down. "Let's be on our way. We've wasted enough time."

Asdelar mounted his own horse and gave Hinego an odd sidelong glance. "What is it with you Reds and your unwillingness to talk about yourselves? Almost every member of the Imalt-wor I've ever met has been insufferably stoic."

Hinego leapt into his saddle lightly and twitched the reins to start his mare in the right direction. "And you Blades talk too much," he shot back. "My personal affairs have nothing to do with our current task."

"Don't give me that." Asdelar urged his horse forward so that he was riding beside him. "Look, we're going to be stuck together for gods know how long. Don't you think we should get to know each other a little better? If nothing else, talking will help pass the time."

"You have a map and a limited idea of what the landscape of your own country looks like," Hinego said a trifle snidely. "If you're bored, why don't you study it?"

Asdelar refused to let the taunting get to him. Besides, it only infuriated Hinego more when he kept his own cool. "There's no need to be so catty about it," he remarked, which got exactly the reaction he'd anticipated.

"*Catty*?" Hinego glared at him darkly. "Women are 'catty', Lorem," he spat. "I am merely suggesting you use your brain rather than your mouth for once."

That was an opening Asdelar simply could not pass up. "Talking isn't all I can do with my mouth, you know." And he smiled suggestively for good measure.

Hinego predictably began sputtering in shocked affront, though the faint coloring to his cheeks was an unexpected bonus.

He let the insults go on for a few moments before giving a short laugh and waving a hand dismissively in the air. "Don't get your feathers ruffled, Idra. I'm not foolish enough to tangle with a Red, on the field or off it."

Hinego flung him a scorching glare and urged his horse into a trot, leaving his laughing companion behind.

Chapter Two

Hinego steadfastly refused to participate in any conversation for the rest of the afternoon, even managing to ignore Asdelar's teasing.

Asdelar was not used to being dismissed or disliked, but after his initial sulking, the mind-numbing boredom took the edge off the sting.

While he was loathe to give Hinego the satisfaction of following his advice, he had been correct in his assumption of Asdelar's ignorance. What little he knew of the world outside the city walls was appallingly lacking. Aside from the village he'd been born in, he had done almost no traveling and always relied on guides once he was off the familiar main road that led to the palace and the surrounding city of Oneth.

Asdelar had some difficulty with the map at first; his horse did not appreciate being used as a tabletop, and the breeze occasionally tried to tug the parchment from his hands. Eventually he got the hang of it, holding the map upright with both hands and trusting his horse to follow Hinego's mare. He probably made a funny sight, holding a parchment in the air and gazing at it intently rather than watching the road, but in a few moments he was so absorbed in his scrutiny of the map that he no longer cared.

He had always been vaguely aware that Predala

was a small country, but it looked even smaller when sketched out on a scrap of parchment. He found Oneth easily, as it was nestled in a valley close to the Rockspire Mountains, and from there he tried unsuccessfully to guess their route. The names of towns were jotted down beside the red marks that indicated their location, but villages were written off as simple X's, and their names were not provided. There were many more X's than red marks, so perhaps the mapmaker had just not seen the point. There were three different villages close to Oneth, any one of which might have been his birthplace. There was the King's Road, bold and long. From there he found the smaller road that branched out towards the Lar-Quarl River, which he remembered passing their second day on the road. But after that he was lost.

Asdelar noted with interest that the further south one went, the fewer towns and rivers there were that were named in the old tongue. He'd been taught that many places had been renamed after the fall of the Oneth-far regime, but it was still a little odd to see so many southern rivers with such mundane names as Wildgrass and Catseye. In Oneth many streets, guilds, and even titles were still old Onethian, much like the sects of the King's Gravemen.

His mouth tugged into a deep frown, eyes skimming the inky terrain. In the jumble of villages, rivers, hills, and lakes, he could not for the life of him guess which road they were currently on or where they were headed.

When he glanced up, he caught Hinego looking back at him strangely. He must have read the confusion on Asdelar's face, because he gestured ahead of them, indicating their direction. "Hilstram's not far from here; we should be there by tonight if we hurry. It will take a few days more before we reach the Wildgrass River."

Asdelar stared at the map in disbelief. He'd found the town of Hilstram on the map, and the river looked conveniently close. "A few days?" he repeated incredulously. "Surely not. It's right near the town!"

Hinego frowned at him, then seemed to understand. He adopted a tolerant expression. "Of course. You've never walked a mile, so I suppose I shouldn't expect you to grasp just how far we have to go."

Asdelar frowned right back, embarrassed by his own ignorance but offended by Hinego's condescending attitude. "I run three miles every day."

"Laps around the palace ground don't count."

"I don't think I like your tone, friend."

"That's too bad," Hinego said heartlessly. "And I'm not your friend."

~~*

It was almost too dark to ride safely when at last they topped a slight rise and spotted the lights of Hilstram below.

Hinego seemed familiar with the place, so Asdelar allowed him to take the lead as they entered the town and went down the main street. The town was small but in good repair, though the wooden buildings either side of the street looked so much alike it was as if they had been cut from the same mold.

"This whole place is one big fire hazard," Asdelar

muttered in disapproval. "Don't these people know how to build with stone?"

"It's expensive and time consuming to cart rocks from a quarry so far," Hinego pointed out. "Oneth just happens to be close to an abundant source. Don't expect to see stone buildings anywhere but in cities."

He led them to the inn, and Asdelar hid a slight wince as he dismounted and handed his reins over to the waiting stable boy. He was not used to so many hours in the saddle, and envied Hinego's stamina.

The inn was drab and small compared to Oneth's, but it was well-lit and the smell of roasted meat was strong and appealing as he followed Hinego indoors. "Get a table," Hinego said, glancing around and judging the atmosphere. "I'll set up our rooms."

Too tired to argue about taking or giving orders, Asdelar found an empty table, sturdy and strangely low to the ground, and eased himself onto a short stool.

A tired looking woman in an apron came over after a moment, hair disheveled and hands wrinkled from hours spent washing dishes. "What can I get you, sir?"

Asdelar smiled up at her. "My friend and I could do with something to eat, if it's not too much trouble. And ale, if you have it."

Her face sharpened with renewed interest as she looked him over more carefully, her tone becoming a bit friendlier as his charming smile took effect. "There's some roast left on the fire, and I think we still have some potatoes. I'll get your ale." She arched a brow, eyes lingering on the sword at his hip. "I'm assuming you can pay."

"Of course." He drew his money pouch out of his

vest and jingled it encouragingly, offering another smile. "Thank you, dear."

She couldn't seem to help but smile back girlishly before she hurried off.

Hinego joined him at the table a moment later, his expression less than happy. "Are you as stupid as you look?" he demanded.

Asdelar gave him a cool look, interlacing his fingers on the tabletop. "Are you trying to start a fight?"

"Don't go waving your money about in public like that," Hinego snapped quietly. "That's just asking to get robbed."

Asdelar glanced around quickly at the other patrons, but no one seemed to be paying the least bit of attention to them. "You're being paranoid."

"I'm being prudent," Hinego corrected. "You don't look like a Blade anymore, remember? There's nothing to keep a desperate thug from making a go at you."

"You're here," Asdelar pointed out. "I may not look the part, but no one in their right mind would mess with a Red."

Hinego rolled his eyes. "For now. But don't come crying to me if you get unwelcome visitors in your room tonight."

Asdelar leaned forward, gazing sternly at him. "All right, let's be blunt with each other, shall we? Let's just get it all out in the open and be done with it. Obviously you have a problem with me, which to me is unacceptable if we're going to be expected to work well together. Why don't we just agree to forgive each other our faults and act like civilized human beings?"

Hinego blinked, startled, but found his voice

quickly. "You're asking a Red to be blunt." It wasn't quite a question.

Asdelar frowned. "Yes. You've been borderline rude up until now, so I find it hard to believe you can get much worse."

Hinego's eyes narrowed. He leaned forward as well, an aggressive move that put their faces inches apart. His voice was low and angry. "All right. I think you're a careless, ignorant boy who's more interested in seducing everything that breathes than in doing his job. You're slowing me down and you refuse to take anything seriously."

Asdelar's lips curved in a grim smile, his voice equally quiet but laced with a note of mocking cheer. "I think you're an arrogant, short-tempered know-it-all who's a little too fond of making snap judgments and looking down on everyone from his high horse. You let yourself get angry too quickly, and have the patience of a child."

They glared at each other for a long moment.

Abruptly Asdelar leaned back, all traces of animosity gone. "There. Feel better?"

Hinego peered at him narrowly. "I've fought men for less," he pointed out.

"I believe you."

Hinego grunted and looked away. "Now that we've made it perfectly clear just how much we loathe each other, you just expect us to get along? You're crazier than I thought."

It was Asdelar's turn to roll his eyes. "You're insufferable, Idra. But I don't loathe you. You strike me as the kind of person who takes some getting used to, that's all. You were hand-picked for this job, same as I, so I'm assuming you know what you're doing and you can handle yourself in a fight. You need to trust me to do the same."

Hinego shot him a quick glance, but just then their food arrived, so any further bickering was stalled. They dug into their meals with a will, hungry from a long day of riding. "I've asked for a bath to be drawn," Hinego mumbled around a mouthful of hot potato. "And trust me, we could both use one."

Asdelar opened his mouth for an automatic response, then shut it again when Hinego shot him a warning look. "Don't even say it, Blade."

Asdelar offered a slightly sheepish grin. "Am I that predictable?"

"You seem to find sexual innuendo in almost anything," Hinego noted grimly. He pointed his dinner knife at the other man. "And your reputation as a promiscuous man precedes you. You can have the bath *after* I'm done with it."

"Promiscuous. I suppose that's one word for it," Asdelar agreed.

"I could think of others that seem a bit more fitting," Hinego grumbled.

"But a little less polite, I take it."

Hinego finished his meal first and retreated upstairs for his bath. Asdelar ordered another ale and made his way over to the benches by the hearth where a few men were discussing the latest news.

They acknowledged his approach with slight nods, and he eased himself onto a bench close to the wall so he could lean his back against the bricks warmed by the fire. He gazed into the hearth, sipping his ale and keeping one ear on the discussion.

Most of it was dull: the weather, the occasional road bandit, a local marriage.

"What about you, friend?"

He glanced up to find them both studying him and his sword curiously. "You come down here from further north?"

Asdelar nodded, taking another sip of the ale. It was better than the sludge from the last village, but not by much. "Aye."

"Any news?"

He paused for effect, as if considering it. "There are rumors that the Duke of Thurul's daughter has pulled another disappearing act."

One of the men, hair shot with gray, gave a snort of derisive amusement. "That brat's always runnin' away, as I hear it. One of these days she's gonna find herself in a right pickle."

The other man was tall and skinny as a twig. "I hear she's quite a beauty," he put in. "Hair the color of fire, they say."

"Aye, and a heart as black as night," his companion drawled, unimpressed. "From what I hear, she's a spoilt little brat. Have you ever met her, sir?" His eyes lingered on Asdelar's sword.

Asdelar smiled. "Not me, friend. Though I've heard similar tales of her beauty—and her less than sunny disposition. I hear she usually hides out in villages when she runs off. Wouldn't that be something if she showed up here?"

"That's news to me," the gray-haired man snorted. "I can't imagine someone like her lowering 'erself to such a place." He glanced around the room with an expression of fondness mingled with disgust. "Too dirty and poor for a lady. She'd stand out like a sore thumb. There's nothing this side of the river for someone like her. I'd expect to find her someplace more like Amsdale."

Asdelar carefully kept his tone neutral. "Why's that?"

The man shrugged, taking a long draft of his ale. "It's a sight nicer than this place, that's for damned sure. There's a rumor that the Duke's got family there. Or at least some fool there likes to claim to be related to His Grace. He's probably just trying to make himself sound more important."

"Who would want to associate themselves with Lady Valera?" Asdelar asked in an amused tone. "If she's as horrid as everyone claims, I mean."

The man grinned in agreement. "Most sane men wouldn't, but Sheidach has never been known for his common sense. He's sharp as they come when it has to do with selling goods, but that's about as far as smarts go with that one."

Asdelar laughed and steered the conversation towards trade. By then he had noticed the sidelong glances he was earning from a trio of men seated at a table in the shadows, and watched them out of the corner of his eye.

He spoke with the men another half hour for appearance's sake, then excused himself and ascended the stairs. He chanced a casual glance over his shoulder, feigning interest in the serving girl. The group in the shadows was still watching him covertly.

Hinego's room was adjacent to his, and he rapped on the door loudly.

After a moment the door swung open, and Hinego stepped aside to allow him entrance, running his fingers absently through his wet hair to dry it. Asdelar stepped inside, looking him over discreetly. He had already changed into a light sleeping shirt and a clean pair of trousers. The material clung to skin that hadn't been dried thoroughly, sharply defining the firm muscles along Hinego's chest and shoulders.

Hinego nodded towards the wooden tub. "There's a bit of soap left, though the water's not very warm by now. Just how long did you plan on staying down there?"

"Long enough." Asdelar unbuckled his belt and set it and his sword on a stool close to the tub. "I think I may have gotten a bit of interesting information." He tried to recall the image of the map he'd studied. "Is there a town across the river called Amsdale?"

Hinego frowned at him curiously. "Yes, it's about a two-day ride after we cross the Wildgrass. Why?"

"There's a trader there by the name of Sheidach who claims to be related to Duke Stimad. Do you think she could have headed there?"

"Assuming this isn't a kidnapping, you mean." Hinego crossed his arms over his chest, thinking. "It's worth looking into," he admitted after a moment. "We're headed in that direction anyhow." He arched a brow. "I hope you were subtle about it."

"I was the soul of discretion," Asdelar assured him mockingly, undoing the buttons down the front of his vest.

Hinego snorted quietly, but didn't argue. "I'm going to check on the horses while you're bathing. I doubt the stables here offer much more than stale hay and water, and I'd like to make sure my mare hasn't picked up any burrs or stones in her hooves."

"You can stay," Asdelar offered, all innocence. "I wouldn't want to keep you out of your own room."

Hinego ignored him, already heading out of the

room.

Asdelar grinned to himself and finished stripping. He winced as he sank into the shallow tub. The water was barely even room temperature any more. He bathed as quickly as he could, using up the last of the oily soap. He dried himself off a bit and dressed quickly, not bothering to button up again. He was bending over to retrieve his belt and scabbard when a faint clicking sound reached his ears.

A moment later the lock popped and the door burst open. The three men from downstairs stood in the doorway wielding rough cudgels.

Asdelar straightened, expression stern. "I don't recall inviting you in."

The one in front grinned nastily, showing off yellowed teeth. "Oh, lissen to the nice noble brat. If you know what's good for ya, you'll hand over the money, boy."

Asdelar's sword was out of its sheath in an instant, the slender blade pointed unwaveringly at the would-be thieves. He fell back into a relaxed but ready guard position, a cold smile playing at his lips. "I'm afraid I can't do that, friend."

They looked decidedly nervous at the sign of resistance, but the one in front bared his teeth boldly. "It's three against one, fool. Do you really think you can take us all on?" He hefted his cudgel threateningly.

"If you insist on fighting, I'll be forced to defend myself," Asdelar said with mocking regret. "Though three men with firewood don't pose much of a challenge." He gave a little flick of his blade in invitation. "Who's first? Come on, don't be shy."

The other two looked even more uncertain,

clearly intimidated by his confidence.

"It's three against one, you cowards," the first one shouted angrily. "Rush 'im!"

With wild cries they leapt forward, makeshift clubs lifting aggressively.

Asdelar didn't hesitate or retreat as they had hoped. He shifted his weight forward, arm already swinging in a strong, precise move.

Thump!

The first man found himself staring stupidly at the stump of wood in his hand, the other half of the rough club rolling across the floor.

Two more quick flicks of the blade, and two of the men were stumbling back, howling in pain as blood leaked from the deep gashes across their chests. One final twist and flip, and the last of the bandits nearly wet himself as the sword tip swept before his eyes, nicking the end of his pointed nose.

What little bravado they had deserted them at such a startling turn of speed and skill, and they fled like rabbits.

He watched them go with a disappointed frown, lowering his sword. "Not even enough for a warm-up," he grumbled.

Hinego appeared in the doorway, looking over his shoulder with mild curiosity. He stopped just inside the room and glanced from the shorn-off cudgel on the floor to the drawn sword. "It seems to me like there's an 'I told you so' in order," he mused.

Making a face at him, Asdelar retrieved his scabbard and sheathed the slim sword. "All right, you don't have to act so smug about it. A lesson is learned; isn't that the important thing? I won't go waving my money about so carelessly in the future."

"You didn't kill them."

Asdelar stared at him. "Of course not! They were just common thieves and not too bright at that. They just needed a bit of a scare. They won't be a problem any longer."

"They won't bother *you*," Hinego agreed, striding over to his bed. "That doesn't mean they won't go looking for less challenging prey after they're done licking their wounds. If you hadn't the stomach to execute them, you could have rounded them up and handed them over to me; I have the authority to make arrests. And executions for that matter."

Asdelar shook his head. "They're long gone by now. Besides, there's no honor in slaughtering desperate peasants."

Hinego gave him a long look, then gestured towards the door. "Just try to get some sleep. We have another early start in the morning. And Blade..."

Asdelar hesitated just outside the threshold, turning in query to meet Hinego's hard gaze.

"Don't let your conscience get in the way of self-preservation. Our mission is more important than the lives of some no-good criminals."

"Perhaps it's better that Blades have been 'sheltered' at the palace, as you call it," Asdelar noted. "It gives us more appreciation for human life."

Hinego walked over and shut the door in his face.

Chapter Three

Asdelar had hoped that after their honesty with each other over dinner at the inn his sullen companion would open up a bit more, but he was disappointed.

The three days it took to reach the Wildgrass were filled with silence interspersed with snide comments that usually resulted in more arguments. Asdelar found their fights amusing for the most part, perhaps because Hinego was so easily baited. But Hinego's scorn for him only grew.

It was late afternoon when they reached their destination, and they dismounted to let their horses drink.

"So this is the Wildgrass," Asdelar said, watching the rushing water a bit apprehensively. "Are we really going to cross this? It looks a bit risky."

"We won't cross here," Hinego said, pointing upriver. "There should be a ford further up. Let the horses rest first. Even at the ford the water's pretty choppy in spring."

They ate a late lunch while their horses grazed, then walked their mounts upriver for half a mile until Hinego stopped and jerked his chin towards the river. "There it is. It's shallow here." He frowned, looking from the bank to the water. "There's usually a rope pegged down on each bank to make the crossing a bit easier." He moved about, kicking at the grass until his leather boot sought out the worn peg in the ground. He bent over and lifted an old rope. He began pulling on the slack line, and Asdelar's eyebrows rose as it came slithering out of the water to rest in the grass by his feet.

"It seems it broke."

Hinego's frown deepened as he inspected the other end of the rope. "No. It looks like it's been cut. There isn't enough of it to carry all the way across."

Asdelar was puzzled. "You think someone deliberately cut it? Who would do that?"

"Someone who doesn't want to be followed," Hinego muttered, toeing off his boots and rolling up his trousers. He wrapped his nervous mare's reins around his hand and waded into the water. "Perhaps we're on the right trail. Come on."

Asdelar mimicked his actions, lashing boots and sword firmly to the saddle before tugging his own reluctant horse into the gurgling river. "It's cold," he gasped, hesitating just a few feet in.

Hinego sent an impatient glare over his shoulder, shouting to be heard above the sound of the water. "Move it, Blade. It's not a good idea to stop in the middle of the ford. The spring rains have made the water rise, and if you lose your footing you're lost."

Clenching his teeth, Asdelar obediently followed.

The water was cold as ice, and in a matter of minutes his feet were completely numb. At least, he comforted himself, he could no longer feel the river rocks digging into the soles of his feet.

The water was just below knee level at first, but it tugged against his legs with surprising force. It was easy to move against for the first few yards, until they got closer to the middle of the river and the water quickly got deeper.

Asdelar cursed as the icy chill of the water swept up his body and seeped through his clothing. He almost stopped to catch his bearings, but the current was much stronger than it had been by the bank, and it was difficult to keep his balance. Digging his toes into the uneven bottom, he forced himself onwards. The water was nearly chest deep now, and he could feel his horse shuddering from cold and fear through the reins held taut between them. He kept his eyes firmly on Hinego's back, unclenching his teeth just long enough to shout, "Is it going to get much deeper?"

Hinego turned his head slightly to respond, and then suddenly he wasn't there anymore.

Asdelar stared in shock, hesitating despite himself. The river immediately seized him, trying to sweep his feet out from under him, and he lunged for his horse, wrapping an arm around the strong neck and digging his feet into the river bottom. Once he had his balance again he looked around quickly for Hinego.

Hinego's mare was straining against the hard pull of her reins, and a moment later Hinego's head burst above the water. He struggled to regain his feet, coughing and sputtering. His horse dug all four feet in and became his anchor as he dragged himself upwards with the reins. Asdelar watched with his heart in his throat. Water that lapped at his shoulders was nearly at Hinego's chin, and he seemed to be finding it a lot more difficult to find and keep his balance. It didn't help that they were now in the middle of the river, where the current was strongest.

For a moment it looked as if Hinego was going to right himself, but then an undercurrent snatched at him, dragging him down again. His shout was nearly drowned in the roar of the river as he disappeared from view again.

"Hinego!"

Asdelar released his horse's neck and let the water force him away from the animal the length of the reins. He looked about quickly, heart pounding as he struggled to catch a glimpse of cloth or hair. A splash to his left jerked his attention in that direction.

Hinego had resurfaced farther down the river, too far away to get back to his horse. The current had him, and though he was swimming strongly, he could not fight the water. Faintly, a litany of bloodcurdling curses floated its way upriver to Asdelar.

"Hinego!" Asdelar didn't hesitate. He forced himself toward his horse, clinging to the saddle. Yanking at his scabbard, he left the blade tied and swung the leather case hard against his startled horse's flank. The frightened stallion surged forward, nearly running into the mare. Confused and afraid, both horses made their way towards the far shore.

Asdelar took a deep breath, released the reins, and let the river pull his feet out from under him. He went under immediately, and for a moment panic almost set in. The river was impossibly strong and ruthless, dragging him along the bottom before buffeting him along, spinning and turning, unable to guess which way was up or down. It took all his strength to break the surface, and he gasped in great gulps of air when his head broke above the water.

It was easier to swim downriver with the current, but more difficult to keep his head above water as he kicked strongly.

Hinego had been pulled even farther downstream, and his struggles seemed to be weakening.

Gritting his teeth in an attempt to keep the water out of his mouth, Asdelar sliced at the water with his arms, encumbered by the scabbard and limbs that were numb from the cold.

The river was merciless, and Hinego had quite a head start. Things might have turned out for the worst if not for the rocks.

Further down from the ford the bottom grew even rockier, and some of the rocks were just large enough to peep above the water. The current slammed Hinego into one of them, and he scrabbled at it, but the water tore his fingers away. He had better luck with the next one as he shot just alongside it, and managed to catch hold of the uneven surface. He clutched the rock with white-tipped fingers, arms visibly shaking with the effort as the river tugged at him, trying to tear him free. His grip wouldn't hold for long, and Asdelar increased his efforts despite his exhaustion.

He wasn't sure exactly what he was going to do, but the river ended up practically making his decision for him.

Asdelar crashed into the rock with enough force to drive all the air out of his lungs, and he might have gone under if the water hadn't pinned him so firmly in place. He reached across the rock and seized Hinego's shirt sleeve, attempting to drag him around the rock. Straining to lever himself away from the rock, he reached for his other hand.

Then he was being snatched away from the rock,

and water rushed into his mouth, silencing his shout of dismay.

Moments later he resurfaced, coughing and shaking his head to clear the water from his eyes. Amazingly, he had kept his grip on Hinego's sleeve, and now they were both being swept downstream.

"Idiot!" Hinego sputtered, reaching out desperately and latching onto his arm to strengthen their hold. "Now we'll both be killed!"

Asdelar barely heard him. They were coming up on a dead tree that had fallen into the river, its twisted branches extending nearly to the middle of the river. Its trunk lay on the far bank. It was a slim chance, but one Asdelar was too desperate to pass up. He wrestled against the water's pull and managed to lift his scabbard. "Hang on to me!" he shouted.

Hinego's response was garbled, and Asdelar was too busy watching the approaching tree to decipher it. Strong arms wrapped around his torso like a vise.

They were going to pass right by the crown of the tree. There would be no second chances. Asdelar waited with tension singing in his veins as they flew towards it, scabbard upheld.

Now–

"Hold on!" he shouted, and swung the sturdy leather case at a narrow junction between two thick limbs, putting all his remaining strength behind the blow.

At first he thought he'd missed, as they started to sweep past the tree—but the case was wedged firmly, and jerked them to a stop so suddenly he was afraid his arm would be torn out.

Hinego was nearly ripped away from him, but he clung to Asdelar desperately, gasping at the strain, expression one of numb surprise.

Their strength was nearly gone, but hope and desperation gave them both an extra boost, and they dragged themselves along the twisted branches with shaking arms.

It felt like it took hours, but it could only have been a few minutes. Asdelar's limbs were so numb he didn't even feel his feet drag the bottom, but a moment later his knee scraped against the shore, and he knew they were safe.

The current wasn't as strong along the bank's edge, and both men fell to their hands and knees, crawling their way painfully out of the water and up onto the grassy bank. The moment they were on dry ground they collapsed, shaking with fatigue.

Asdelar lay with his face in the grass, panting for air. He turned his head just enough to check on Hinego, who was stretched on his side, coughing roughly to rid his lungs of water.

They were alive.

It took a very long time for some of their strength to return and that was when they both became aware of how bone-chillingly cold they were.

Asdelar's teeth were chattering so hard his skull ached, but he forced his trembling limbs to obey, and managed to get up on unsteady feet. "We n-n-need a f-fire," he managed to say through numb lips.

Hinego rolled onto his stomach, lifting his head at a faint whinny. His mare was trotting their way, with Asdelar's stallion following doggedly.

"Thank the gods," Asdelar breathed, stumbling over and catching their reins. Hinego struggled to his own feet and staggered over to stroke his mare's nose fondly.

"Good girl," he murmured.

Asdelar dug through his saddlebags until he found his bag of flint and tinder, thankfully still dry.

"We need to f-find somewhere d-d-dry," Asdelar said, looking around.

"The horses first," Hinego insisted, hands clumsy with cold as he pulled a rough blanket out of his own bag. "Unless you want them c-collapsing. They're as cold as w-we are."

They rubbed both shivering horses down roughly with the blankets until circulation had started again, then moved further away from the river. By the time they had managed to collect enough firewood and set up a hasty camp, the sky was already darkening. They changed into dry clothes and laid their soaking shirts and trousers out in the grass near the fire.

They sat as close to the fire as they could stand, wrapped in their blankets and waiting for their shaking to lessen. Neither man had the strength or willpower to even consider dinner, and for almost an hour they sat in weary silence, rubbing at their exhausted, frozen limbs and waiting for the warmth of the fire to seep in.

"This might work better if we helped each other," Asdelar finally pointed out, trying a smile on for size. It felt weak and lopsided.

Hinego shot him a sharp glance, but didn't respond. After a long moment he finally got to his feet and moved around the fire to sit down beside Asdelar. They maneuvered their blankets until their bodies were pressed against each other.

Asdelar gave a small sigh of relief as some of Hinego's body heat slowly seeped through his clothes, warming his side.

"You're an idiot," Hinego declared quietly, staring at the fire without expression.

Asdelar laughed weakly. "So you've said before."

Hinego looked at him out of the corner of his eye for a moment, then returned his tired gaze to the fire. "Thank you," he mumbled grudgingly.

Asdelar gave a one-shouldered shrug, blinking heavily. "You would have done the same for me," he pointed out. "You strike me as an honorable man, if a bit of an infuriating one."

Hinego snorted quietly, but his mouth twitched in the beginnings of a smirk.

Asdelar had every intention of making his own makeshift bed in the grass once he got some strength back, but Hinego was a comforting warm weight against him, and exhaustion made keeping his eyes open nearly impossible.

He was asleep moments later.

Chapter Four

It was birdsong that woke Hinego at sunrise; the familiar noise was one that often roused him on his travels with the other Imalt-wor.

Waking up pressed against another body was not, however, commonplace. He checked his initial hasty retreat, remaining still as his eyes darted around, taking in his surroundings while his sleep-fogged brain put together the pieces.

Cold ashes from a fire that they had foolishly neglected to bank during the night. His mare grazing sedately nearby with a stallion. Limbs that had grown stiff from being in an awkward position for hours. The only part of him that was warm, despite the blanket, was his right side, which was pressed up against the aforementioned body.

Craning his eyes upwards, he caught a glimpse of golden hair, and relaxed his tensed muscles a bit as memories finally slipped free out of the confusion.

The river. Asdelar saving him. Sitting together for body heat. Exhaustion must have won over them both, and they had fallen asleep propped against each other. Unfortunately, Hinego's head had dropped onto Asdelar's shoulder in slumber, which was not only embarrassing but was guaranteed to leave him with a painful strain in his neck for most of the day. Likewise, Asdelar head was currently using his as a pillow, and any movement would surely awaken him.

Hinego gave a small huff of annoyance and tried to remain as still as possible. The other man was warm, and the morning was chilly.

Hinego's unfriendly feelings about him aside, Asdelar had risked his life in going after Hinego in the river. He was grateful, but not entirely happy about the fact. Hinego didn't like feeling like he owed anybody anything.

He stayed where he was for several minutes, a bit unwilling to wake his exhausted companion. But eventually his stomach began loudly reminding him that neither of them had bothered to make dinner last night. Besides, he needed to get the fire started. He shrugged off his blanket and pulled away from his slumbering companion.

An arm snaked out, wrapping around his waist and holding him in place. Asdelar mumbled, head bobbing, but his balance was thrown off. Still half asleep, he slouched over onto his side, pulling Hinego down with him and nearly crushing him.

"Lorem!" Hinego snapped, pulling at the strong arm holding him so firmly in place. How could the buffoon still be asleep? "Let go of me, idiot. It's morning."

Asdelar's nose crinkled and he muttered unintelligibly before rolling over abruptly and practically burrowing himself against Hinego's body, seeking warmth. "Hnnf." Hinego shivered involuntarily as a cold nose pressed against his throat. "Jus' a few more minutes ..."

Scandalized and flustered, Hinego jabbed him none-too-gently in the stomach with his elbow.

"Lorem! Wake up, damn you! And get your hands off of me before I break both your arms. I'm not one of your whores."

Asdelar finally opened his eyes, blinking slowly in confusion on coming face-to-face with Hinego's dark scowl. "Hunh? Wha?" Finally comprehension dawned, his blue eyes coming into sharp focus. He pulled his arm away and sat up quickly. "Oh—Idra. Sorry about that."

Hinego muttered an impolite response under his breath and climbed to his feet, carefully stretching the kinks out of his body. "You sleep like the dead," he grumbled, moving away to start the fire. "Do something useful and get me some tinder, unless you want a cold breakfast."

Asdelar winced, reaching up to rub ruefully at the back of his neck. "Gods, I feel like someone beat me with a club."

"We fell asleep sitting up," Hinego said over his shoulder, digging through his pack for food. "Stretch your muscles or you won't even be able to stay in your saddle."

Asdelar got to his feet slowly and began a slow circle of the camp, pulling up dead grass and twigs for tinder.

There were still some hot coals underneath the remains of the previous night's firewood, so it didn't take long to get a fire started. Asdelar would have preferred a leisurely breakfast, his muscles still sore and cramped, but Hinego ate quickly and immediately began going through a series of stretches and warm-ups to get his blood flowing.

"Someone cut that rope," he pointed out, doing a few squats. "It could just be bandits on the run, or it could be something more. The fact that we still haven't heard any word about Lady Valera makes it hard to dismiss foul play."

"If she's as temperamental as I've heard, I almost pity the men who took her." Asdelar stuffed the last of his toasted bread in his mouth and got to his feet painfully. "Ouch. I don't think I can ride."

"That's got to be a first for you," Hinego muttered, stretching his arms over his head and leaning to the left to stretch the muscles in his side.

Asdelar froze in the act of popping the kinks out of his back, hands pressed to his lower back as he stared at the other man incredulously. "Holy gods, he's grown a sense of humor. Idra, I'm so proud of you. You made your first sexual joke."

"Shut the hell up, Blade," Hinego snapped, turning his back on him and rolling the stiffness out of his shoulders. There was a noticeable lack of hostility in his tone, however, and Asdelar chose to take it as a good sign.

They had ended up further downstream than they'd originally intended, so it was another hour before they found the main road again. They spent the first few minutes riding in silence before Asdelar seemed to come to some sort of decision and nudged his horse up to ride alongside Hinego's mare.

"I've been thinking," he started.

"That can't be good."

"Oh, don't be so peevish. Anyway, it occurs to me that we've been on the road together almost, what, six days now? And who can tell how much longer we'll be traveling. Even if we find the Duke's daughter in Amsdale, you said it's a two-day ride just to get there. And then there's the trip back."

"Thank you for reiterating the obvious," Hinego grumbled, squinting up at the sky and checking automatically for his hawk. "Is there a point to all of this?"

"My point is that we know almost nothing about each other. I'm not suggesting we be lifelong pals or anything like that, but if you look at it from a warrior's point of view, don't you think that's a bit risky?"

Hinego flicked him a hooded sideways glance, but didn't respond.

"For instance..." Asdelar rested his hand on the hilt of his sword. "Your fighting style is obviously quite a bit different from mine. I'm a swordsman. You, however, are with the Imalt-wor, and you'll be relying on no weapon if we find ourselves with our backs against the wall, so to speak." Hinego's expression turned cankerous, and Asdelar held up a hand to forestall any argument. "I'm not insulting you, Red. All I'm saying is I've been trained to fight with other swordsmen. More specifically, I've been trained to work and complement the fighting style of other Blades." He lifted his hands to show his ignorance. "If we get cornered, we're both going to be pretty much on our own; we'll just get in each others' way because our styles of fighting are so completely different."

Hinego arched one thin eyebrow. "And this is just now occurring to you?" He sighed in defeat when Asdelar frowned unhappily at him. "Fine. Yes, you're right, we aren't trained to fight together. I know nothing of swordplay. I suppose there's the risk of me unintentionally getting in the path of your sword. And I don't want a leg chopped off because I move quicker or jump higher than you're expecting."

Asdelar laughed.

Hinego was unamused. "There's no way to adapt our fighting styles to each other in so short a time. We'll simply have to try as best we can to stay out of each other's way." He paused, frowning slightly and gazing off into the distance. "There is something else hindering us," he finally admitted grudgingly.

Asdelar smiled. "You mean the fact that we can barely stand each other? Hard to fight with a man who might or might not watch your back."

Hinego grunted in agreement. "That, too. But it's also the simple fact that we know next to nothing about each other on a basic level. Normally I would just observe you during fights and learn how to move around you that way. Obviously we don't have that luxury."

"Then what do you suggest?"

"Faew-bor."

"Pardon?"

"It's an Imalt-wor tactic." Hinego reached into his pocket and procured a red bandanna the same shade as the sash about his chest, tying it around his forehead to keep his hair out of his face and give his eyes a bit of shade. It was getting warmer, and Asdelar was for once grateful that he was not wearing his prized armor. "Basically it means 'learning the inner thoughts'."

"Ummm ..." Asdelar scratched at the stubble that was beginning to sprout on his chin, making a mental note to shave as soon as he had a decent mirror. "You've lost me, I'm afraid."

"It's a fancy way of saying getting to know each other," Hinego said tersely. "As you said, you Blades are taught to think and act together as one massive group. That's the opposite of how the Imalt-wor train.

We are expected to be able to fight individually so each man can take out as many opponents as possible." He paused, collecting his thoughts as he decided how best to explain it. "If you put five men through the exact same training for the exact same amount of time, you will still not have five equally talented fighters. There is bound to be one who is weaker than the others, and one who surpasses his fellows. For the Blades, this is hardly an issue; there are over a score of you per squad to make up for any one man's weakness. But the Imalt-wor are never all together at one time. We are separated into teams and sent off to various locations. Usually one of our squads consists of anywhere from three to six men and women."

"Women?" Asdelar interrupted, unable to hide his surprise. "I'd heard that there were female Reds, but I've never seen any. I guess there aren't very many."

Hinego rolled his eyes. "Your tone is offensive, Blade. There are over two-score Imalt-wor currently in action; fifteen of them are women. Some of the best fighters I know are these women you seem so surprised over."

Asdelar held up a hand defensively. "I'm not one to mock a Red's fighting ability, male or female," he said quickly. "It's just ... well, I may not know much about how you Reds do business, but I do know it's not exactly an easy life. Constantly on the move, using a fighting style that requires a good deal of strength and concentration ..." He shrugged. "Most of the women I've met seem uninterested in anything other than fashion and politics."

"That's because you've spent all of your adult life inside the city walls, and the Banam-hin is mono-gendered," Hinego snapped. "Perhaps if your commander were not so short-sighted, he would take it upon himself to allow women into the Blade ranks."

Asdelar winced, trying hastily to get back to safer ground. "So these squads, they're small."

Hinego gave him a hard look before continuing. "The Imalt-wor don't have the same pack mentality that you Blades do. Though we are expected to fight as single units, we have to *know* we can trust our comrades to look after themselves; each member must be able to face off against multiple opponents without aid. But each person fights in a slightly different way. We learn our squadmates' strengths and weaknesses in combat as quickly as we can, and that makes everything easier."

"But you've never seen me fight," Asdelar said.

Hinego nodded. "It's not just that I'm unaccustomed to fighting with a swordsman; I don't know how to fight with *you*."

"I don't know, we fight a lot," Asdelar teased.

Hinego offered him a flat look. "I had thought this trip would be brief. However, the more Lady Valera's disappearance looks like a kidnapping, the more likely it will be that we'll end up relying on each other in a fight. You are accustomed to having someone watch your back and I am used to having allies stay out of my way. This could be problematic."

"Are you asking me to duel you or something?"

"No. But if I don't understand you on a basic level, I won't be able to guess what you'll do in battle."

Asdelar straightened in his saddle suddenly. "Are you suggesting we get to learn more about each other on a personal level?" he asked brightly. "It's about time." He hesitated. "Although there is one flaw to your master plan, Idra. Everyone in your squad at least fights basically the same. Learning their individual personalities is just a bonus. While I'm sure this would be helpful for us, it still doesn't cancel out the fact that I fight with the sword and you with your fists. We still risk getting in each other's way."

"Of course." Hinego shrugged. "But for now it's all we have to work with. We don't have time to waste showing off our fighting abilities." At Asdelar's skeptical look, he added, "Do you want proof that it will help?"

Asdelar nodded silently.

"Fine, here's one useful fact I've picked up from you." Hinego pointed at the him almost accusingly. "I know that you would rather spare a man than take his life. Therefore, I know if there's killing to be done, I'm going to have to do it myself. And if a man gets past you, I'll know ahead of time to be ready to take him out before you let him get away."

Asdelar stiffened, eyes narrowing. "If you're referring to that incident at the inn, let me remind you that they were simple, blundering thieves with the intent to rob, not murder, otherwise they would have found something a little more dangerous than pieces of firewood to fight me with. I know how and when to kill a man, Red, but I'm not going to turn my sword on an unarmed opponent. They were defeated; there was no point in killing them in cold blood."

Hinego sneered, looking away dismissively.

Asdelar bit his tongue and reined in his rising temper stubbornly. He would not allow Hinego to drag him into a fight, and he was not going to explain his reasoning to someone who had no intention of listening. He waited until he was sure his voice would be level before speaking again. "All right, so we know nothing about each other. Let's fix that." He shifted in his saddle until he was more comfortable. "Let's start with you. Why are you so unfriendly?"

Hinego stared at him. "Excuse me?" he demanded sharply.

Asdelar gave him a pointed look. "You have got to be the singularly most mistrustful, prickly man I've ever met. I've been the soul of courtesy since we've met, but you act as if you want nothing to do with me whatsoever. If I've offended you somehow, you need to tell me, or we're never going to learn to work together. What exactly is it about me that you find so repulsive?"

"I don't find you 'repulsive'," Hinego retorted, scowling weakly and refusing to meet the other man's penetrating stare. "And haven't we already been over each other's faults?"

"You seem to be relying mostly on rumors," Asdelar pointed out. "Admit it: you'd built your opinion about me before we even met." He grinned. "It makes me wonder what kind of rumors you've been hearing. Am I made out to be some sort of sex god, devoid of morals or scruples?"

"Sex god?" Hinego snorted loudly, cheeks coloring faintly at the topic. "Hardly. But all one has to do is mention your name in passing on the streets of Oneth, and girls sigh and giggle in a fairly annoying manner. Certain men grin rather foolishly, too, for that matter." He sent his partner a level look. "And in just the few days we've been together, you've flirted shamelessly with anyone who shows an interest in you."

Asdelar shrugged, unconcerned. He tried to hide his amusement at Hinego's prudishness without much success. "I assure you I've slept with less people than you assume. I don't go about trying to single-handedly deflower virgins or increase the population, you know. I just enjoy that sort of company and the intimacy that comes with it. I enjoy it, they enjoy it. I see no harm in it as long as I avoid those who are married and ensure the women take a tonic beforehand to prevent any unwanted children." He grinned. "And how about you?"

"Me?"

"Yes, you. This subject obviously makes you uncomfortable. Don't tell me you're a blushing virgin, Idra."

Hinego's glare could have melted lead, but his tone was icy. "Unlike some, I am not so quick to go braying my private matters all over the place. Whether or not I seek such company as that is none of your business or anyone else's."

"You get real formal when your delicate sensibilities have been offended, did you know that?"

And that was the end of any sort of congenial conversation that day.

Chapter Five

Amsdale was a larger town than its neighbor across the Wildgrass.

Personally Asdelar couldn't have cared less. Even after two days, he felt sore from his struggle in the river, and hours on horseback hadn't helped any. He shot Hinego a jealous look. If he was still suffering from their harrowing adventure, it certainly didn't show. The stretches he performed morning and night seemed to have eased off any muscle fatigue. Asdelar made a mental note to have Hinego teach him the trick.

Hinego slid from his saddle once they were on the town's main road and stopped a passing woman. "Excuse me, do you know where we could find a merchant by the name of Sheidach?"

The woman shifted her basket of laundry to her other hip, gesturing down the street. "It's the horrible pink house just down that way. You can't miss it."

"Thank you," Hinego said politely. He looked up at Asdelar after the woman had moved on. "We should get our rooms first and get the horses in a stable."

"I don't suppose we could grab a bite to eat before we go looking for this fashion-challenged merchant?" Asdelar suggested hopefully, climbing down from his horse with a wince.

"Later." Hinego led his mare across the street

towards the town's inn. "First I want to see if Sheidach has any useful information to offer us. If not, it will be a short trip anyhow."

"It's all business with you, isn't it?"

Hinego frowned as if the question was ludicrous. "We're on a mission, Blade."

"Yes, yes, I know. But for gods' sake, Hinego, can't you learn to loosen up even a little bit?" Asdelar held his reins out to the stable boy who came jogging up. He rolled his eyes at Hinego's stern glare. "Fine, let's find this supposed relative of the Duke and get this over with." He turned to frown at the stable boy, who still hadn't taken his horse.

"I'm sorry, sirs," the boy said quickly, "but the inn's full tonight."

"Full?" Hinego looked up from where he'd been unfastening a saddlebag. "Is there any particular reason?"

"There's a carnival passing through, sir. Actually, it's more like a family of performers. They've taken what rooms there were available."

Asdelar gave a huff of annoyance. "Well, is there another inn?"

Hinego shook his head. "Never mind. Is there a Red Cove in town?"

The boy's eyes flitted to the scarlet sash across the man's chest and he nodded. "Yes, sir. It's just down there." He pointed further down the street.

Hinego turned away, giving his complacent mare a tug to get her to follow. "Come on, Lorem."

Asdelar followed, frowning quizzically. "Red Cove?" he repeated.

"It's sort of like a temporary headquarters for the Imalt-wor; most decent-sized towns have them. They cater specifically to Reds passing through for a minimum fee. In return, the owner's taxes are significantly decreased. Most of the supplies you can get there, such as extra uniforms, are also provided by the crown."

"Can a Blade stay there?"

"You're with me. There shouldn't be a problem."

The Red Cove was a small building, squeezed in between the tailor and the blacksmith. The sign over the door was a crude painting of a red sash wrapped around a fist.

Hinego tied his mare to the post outside and went in; Asdelar hastened to follow his lead. The ground floor was a narrow room with two long tables, each able to seat almost a dozen men. There was a low desk in front of the back door leading to the kitchen that seemed to serve as a makeshift bar. The man behind the desk lifted his chin to get their attention, wiping absently at a mug with his apron. His eyes drifted to Hinego's tell-tale sash as the two men walked over. "You need a room?"

"Two, preferably," Hinego answered, fishing coins out of his pouch. "And we have two horses that need a stable, just outside."

The man didn't take the coins right away, eyeing Asdelar up and down. "This one doesn't look like a Red," he grunted.

"He's Banam-hin. He's with me."

The man frowned slightly, but after a moment he gave a small shrug, accepting and pocketing the coins in one quick practiced move. "There's a squad passing through, but we have some rooms available. Take four and five. I'll get my daughter to tend to your horses. Dinner's served at seven."

"Thank you." Hinego turned to head for the door. "Come on, Lorem. Let's go see this boastful merchant."

"I've got a brilliant idea," Asdelar said impudently. "Why don't you try calling me 'Asdelar'? It's really not that difficult to say. And that way you won't sound so damned formal and condescending all the time."

Hinego turned to glare at him in disapproval, but before he could offer a scathing retort, an amused voice spoke up from the other side of the room.

"Idra has made being condescending into an art form. It's no use trying to humanize him. You might as well bang your head against a wall for all the good it will do you."

There was a woman coming down the stairs that led to the upstairs rooms. A dry smile was teasing at her lips. Asdelar did a double-take as he noticed the red sash across her chest.

"Morasa." Hinego looked surprised. "I didn't know your squad was this far south. Weren't you supposed to be stationed in Redor-mal, taking care of that serf uprising?"

"Huh. Some uprising." She strode over, waving her hand dismissively by her shoulder. "A dozen serfs waving pitchforks and doing a whole lot of yelling and not much else. They shut up pretty quick when we arrived, and we had a nice little talk with His Grace. Count Odaro won't be making any more unapproved taxes, I can tell you that." She put her hands on her hips and eyed Asdelar up and down with frank interest. "Who's your friend?"

Hinego gestured between them. "Asdelar Lorem of the Banam-hin. Lorem, this is Morasa Ledyn. Attempt to control your raging libido. She'd probably rip your arms out."

"Maybe not with this one," Morasa mused, smiling impishly at Asdelar.

Asdelar responded with a smile of his own and a sweeping bow. "Charmed, my lady."

"My lady, hah!" she snorted in a decidedly unladylike way. "Isn't he the flatterer? What are you doing rubbing shoulders with a Blade, Hinego?"

"King's orders," Hinego said vaguely. "We're looking for a man named Sheidach."

Morasa arched her brow, not missing his evasion of the question, but let it pass. "Sheidach the merchant? He's a slimy sort of fellow. What could you possibly want with him?"

"That's our business, Morasa."

"Oh, don't get your trousers in a twist, you big stick-in-the-mud. I'll take you to his place. Haven't got anything better to do right now, anyway."

Asdelar found himself studying Morasa out of the corner of his eye as she led them down the street. She was a handsome woman, and she exuded professionalism and confidence. Her dark hair was cropped short, and she walked with her head high and her shoulders back. She was a shade taller than Hinego, and thin and lean as a whip. She was nothing like most of the women Asdelar had ever known; for one, she was dressed in a simple tunic and hose instead of a dress. She was also very forthright and seemed to feel that she was an equal to the two men in her company. Asdelar felt he might come to like her, given enough time to know her better.

She had been filling Hinego in on her time in Redor-mal, but turned to Asdelar abruptly, taking him off guard. "So, tell me a bit about yourself, Lorem. I've rarely had a chance to make conversation with a Blade. On the road too often, you know."

He grinned at her. "Please, call me Asdelar. This is a first for me, as well. I've never actually met a female Red."

"We exist, I assure you," she drawled, amused. "So, Asdelar, you look younger than most Blades I've seen. You must be fairly talented with the sword."

"I'm sure we're the same age, Miss Ledyn. It seems I am merely cursed with a boyish face."

"I'm going to like this one," Morasa informed Hinego. "And Morasa is just fine, Asdelar."

Hinego snorted and muttered something under his breath about her age.

She slapped him in the back of the head calmly. "It's not polite to discuss a woman's age, Idra. I'm barely five years your senior. Don't be a toad. So, Asdelar, who did you irritate to get stuck with old stone-face here? Is he a walking talking stereotype of the Reds or what?"

Asdelar swallowed a laugh when Hinego glared at them both. "It's not like that. I hear he came highly recommended. The King asked us to—"

"Is that it?" Hinego interrupted, pointing.

Morasa came to a halt, lip curling in distaste as she gazed at the building he was indicating. "Oh, yes, that's it all right. Hideous, isn't it?"

"It looks more like mauve than pink," Asdelar said, mildly horrified. "Still, it's not exactly easy on the eyes. It's a rather odd choice of color."

"Sheidach's an odd sort of man," Morasa admitted, walking up to the door and giving it a mild kick.

"Come back tomorrow," a voice called from

inside. "No more business today."

"Open up, Sheidach," Morasa shouted back. "This is Imalt-wor business."

There was a long pause, then the door opened outwards abruptly, forcing her to take a step back. The man who stared out at them was overweight, and Asdelar found his taste in clothing to be as unpleasant as the outside of his house. He glanced at each of them in turn with quick beady eyes, a nervous frown tugging at his mouth. "What's all this about? I haven't done anything wrong. I run a fair business."

Morasa held up her hand sharply. "Save it, Sheidach." She nodded towards Hinego. "We just have some questions for you."

"May we come in?" Hinego asked solemnly. "I would prefer not to discuss this on the street."

Sheidach hesitated, then stepped back, reluctantly allowing them entrance.

Most of the first floor had been converted into a place of business, with crates and sacks piled against the walls. Rugs were laid out for perusal across the floor in a strange patchwork effect, and there were various odds and ends lined up on shelves and scattered around the room.

Sheidach moved his bulk around a handsomely carved cupboard and shuffled over to his desk. He lowered himself into his chair and began shifting paperwork around absently, watching them with a faint air of suspicion. "Er, what can I do for the Imalt-wor? If this is about that misunderstanding with the new trade routes—"

"This is not about your business," Hinego said. "We have some questions regarding the Duke of

Thurul and his family. There is a rumor that you are related to them in some way. Is this true?"

Morasa flicked Asdelar a questioning look, but didn't interrupt.

Sheidach looked confused at the strange question, but a moment later his eyes narrowed shrewdly. "I might be. I don't see how that's anyone's business but my own."

"It seems to be everyone's business," Hinego pointed out coolly. "Apparently you're quite fond of boasting of this alleged relation. I don't like repeating myself, master merchant. Answer the question."

Sheidach leaned back in his chair and laced his fingers over his paunch.

"If the next words out of your mouth are something slippery and witty, let me cut you off right here," Morasa spoke up. "Idra is not a man you want annoyed with you, and I am likewise inclined to take offense to any garbage you might consider spewing. A member of the Imalt-wor just asked you a question. I suggest you answer it."

Sheidach scowled, but finally said grudgingly, "Yes, it's true. You really think I would be stupid enough to claim it if it wasn't? I'm related to the Duke—distantly—on my mother's side."

Hinego nodded. "Then you know his daughter, Lady Valera."

"I know *of* her," Sheidach corrected. "I hear she's a right terror. I don't have anything to do with the family. The relation is too distant and muddied. They probably don't even know I exist. I've never met the girl personally." His gaze sharpened in interest. "Why do you ask, anyway? Has the little snob run off again?"

"Why would you ask that?" Hinego demanded quickly.

Sheidach shrugged. "We're not that far south of Thurul, you know. Everyone knows how she likes to pull her idiotic disappearing tricks and drive the Duke mad with worry. A few years back she was missing longer than usual and the Red squad that was stationed here at the time asked me if I'd seen her." He shook his head. "I'll tell you what I told them. I've never heard of her coming this far south, and even if she did, it would probably never occur to her to seek me out. She wouldn't know of me, and even if she'd heard the same rumors you have, I can't see her lowering herself to asking a simple merchant like myself for any sort of help. I would only turn her in anyway. The King would have me strung up by my toes if I harbored her instead of returning her safely. Everyone knows how he dotes on the brat."

"Watch your mouth," Hinego snapped reflexively. He exchanged a look with Asdelar. "Thank you for your time."

Sheidach made a rude noise in his throat. "I'd show you the door, but I'm sure you can find it yourselves."

Morasa quelled him with a cold look.

Once they were outside again, Asdelar blew out an explosive sigh, raking his hand through his hair. "Another lovely dead end," he grumbled. "Now what do we do?"

"Is that what this is all about?" Morasa asked curiously. "You're looking for the Duke's daughter?"

"She's been missing much longer than usual," Hinego explained. "The King himself is taking over the search. Lorem and I are to find her and bring her back." He frowned, rubbing at the back of his neck in visible frustration. "The rumor about Sheidach's bloodline was the only lead we had, and it was a tenuous one at that."

"There was the rope," Asdelar said.

"Rope?" Morasa repeated blankly.

Hinego shrugged. "Someone cut the rope leading across the ford in the Wildgrass. We'd hoped it was a sign that we were on the right track."

Morasa's eyebrows shot up. "You think she's been kidnapped?"

Hinego glanced around suddenly. "Perhaps this isn't something we should be discussing in public," he said in a quieter tone. "Especially on the off-chance that we *are* on to something."

"Right." Morasa crossed her arms under her breasts and frowned. "So I take it you won't be in town long?"

"There's no point. We can nose about a bit in the morning, but I doubt anything will turn up."

"I'll ask the rest of the squad," Morasa offered. "And I'll keep my ear to the ground. Who knows, maybe something will turn up. In the meantime ..." She grinned at them both pityingly. "If you ask me, you both look like you could use a drink."

Asdelar perked up. "Sounds like a plan."

Hinego scowled at Morasa. "That's your solution to everything. I don't need a drink, I need a bed."

"And someone in it with you, evidently," Morasa drawled. "It might loosen you up some. Gods, man, you haven't changed a bit. I've never seen a man your age wound so tight. It's twenty years too early for you to be such a crotchety fellow."

Hinego leveled her with a dirty look which he

turned on Asdelar when the other man burst out laughing.

"So he's always been this prudish, has he?"

Morasa smirked. "Unfortunately. One can't help but tease him about it. I mean, look at him! Isn't he cute when he's all offended and puffed up?"

Hinego gave a loud sniff that spoke volumes and stalked off, shoulders rigid.

Morasa ran to catch up, laughing. "Oh, come on, Hinego, lighten up. There's nothing else for you to do tonight. Just have a couple of drinks for old time's sake. I haven't seen you in almost two years. We have catching up to do." She latched onto his arm and gently steered him the way she wanted him to go.

"I thought there was a bar back at the Cove," Asdelar said as he fell in step on Hinego's other side.

"Oh gods, trust me, you don't want the ditch water they serve there," Morasa said fervently. "There's a decent pub just down the street. It'll cost more than getting your drinks at the Cove, but at least the taste won't turn your stomach."

"We're going to miss dinner," Hinego protested a bit grumpily. "And aren't you on duty?"

Morasa snorted. "The food's almost as bad as the ale. Besides, Resh and Bonun have the night shift and there's food at the pub. Come on, Hinego, one drink won't kill you."

"... One drink," he finally conceded with bad grace.

"Sure, sure," Morasa said, and sent a secret grin at Asdelar over his head.

Chapter Six

Asdelar smacked his lips in appreciation and lifted his gaze from his fourth—fifth?—ale of the night to offer his brooding companion a hurt look. "So why is it you two are on a first name basis and you can't extend the same courtesy to me?"

Morasa leaned over from where she was seated on Hinego's other side at the bar, grinning at both men. "Oh-ho, that's just Hinego's way of distancing himself from the rest of humanity. Don't take it personally. It took me a year to get him to quit calling me Ledyn."

Hinego scowled into his tankard, visibly displeased with them both. "I said one drink," he mumbled.

"Oh, calm down," Morasa said. "That's only your third, and you're barely sipping at it. Just relax and enjoy yourself, will you? I promise you won't explode. It's pathetic how one has to twist your arm just to get you to have a bit of fun."

The glare that Hinego offered her was slightly off-focus. "I fail to see how drinking oneself into a stupor is considered 'fun'."

Asdelar rolled his eyes. "Three drinks will not have you crawling on the floor," he assured the other man, absently noting the slight slur to his own voice.

"It might," Morasa snickered. She was on her sixth

ale; Asdelar was secretly impressed. "We'll see when he finishes it. Hinego almost never drinks. I shudder to think what he'd be like after five of these."

"How long do you think we have to badger him before we get him that far?"

"Oh, hell, his current buzz will have worn off by the time we manage to talk him into it."

"I hate both of you," Hinego declared sourly.

"You looove us," Morasa said, jostling his arm and causing him to spill a bit. "Now finish that off already. You're nursing it like warm milk. Look, Asdelar's already on his fifth ale. You're making us look bad."

Asdelar lifted his tankard in challenge. "Be a man, Hinego. Are you really going to let a Blade drink you under the table?"

"There are worse places to get a bit drunk," Morasa egged him on. "The ale is good, the atmosphere is friendly, and hey—they've even got music." She gestured vaguely towards the other end of the pub, where two men were playing something jaunty with a wooden flute and drum. "Now drink, Idra, or I'll tell everyone in the squad that you let a Blade get away with badmouthing the Imalt-wor."

Hinego glared at her, but lifted his tankard to his lips. Before Asdelar realized what was happening, Hinego had drained his ale. He slammed the tankard down with excessive force and made a face. "I'm going to regret that in the morning," he said unhappily.

Morasa gave a whoop and clapped him heartily on the shoulder, almost knocking him off his bar stool. "Atta boy!"

"Gods, man!" Asdelar said, inspecting the empty tankard. "Give a guy some warning, will you?" He quickly finished his own ale and bawled for the barkeep.

"No more," Hinego protested. "I said one drink, and that was three. I'm going to bed."

"The hell you are." Morasa seized a fistful of his shirt when he made as if to get down from his stool. She shoved his tankard towards the barkeep for a refill. "Fill 'er up, my good man."

The bartender arched an eyebrow at Hinego, but obliged, filling all three tankards.

"Now take this one as fast as the last, and perhaps we won't heckle you for the rest of the night," Morasa said. "All together, now!"

"Perhaps?" Hinego repeated indignantly. There was a definite slur to his voice now.

"One, two ..." Asdelar said loudly.

Hinego gritted his teeth, but snatched up his own ale and gulped it down along with his companions.

Morasa cheered as three empty tankards rattled against the bar. "That's the spirit, Hinego! Now for some dancing!"

"Dancing?" Hinego repeated, then sputtered an unintelligible protest when she hopped to the ground and dragged him from his stool. Asdelar turned and propped his elbows against the bar to watch, grinning widely.

The musicians spotted the pair and switched tunes to something livelier. Morasa pulled her unwilling dance partner onto the open floor between the tables and began dancing enthusiastically. Hinego was being thoroughly uncooperative, trying to pull out of her grip and stammering protests. He kept stumbling over his own feet, and his face was flushed with embarrassment. The other patrons began hooting and clapping their hands in time to the beat.

Asdelar found his foot tapping along and got to his feet on impulse. Others seemed to have the same idea, and were dragging laughing partners out onto the floor. The drummer found a different beat, and the man on the flute changed his tune to a familiar folk song that had the people on the floor stomping their feet and passing around their dance partners.

Asdelar caught the arm of a woman who came his way, and spun her around before turning to hook elbows with a younger woman and dance a few steps with her. The exercise was rushing the alcohol through his blood quickly, and he felt light-headed and giddy. He had not had the chance to enjoy himself so much in quite a while, and couldn't help but laugh out loud.

He turned to catch the next dance partner, and found his hands settling around a trim but decidedly male waist.

Hinego stumbled against him, face red with embarrassment and exertion. "I don't dance!" he shouted above the noise, trying to push himself away. "Get off of me, you ox."

Asdelar grinned impudently, grabbing one of Hinego's hands and spinning them both around the floor. Hinego nearly lost his footing twice, and was forced to keep up or be dragged along. "Damn you, Lorem, I said get off!"

"Hey, I thought I told you to stop calling me that," Asdelar teased, voice almost drowned out by the music and the cheers of the other dancers. "Relax, Red, I'm not going to tread on your feet. Unless you keep bumbling about like a drunkard."

"I'm not drunk!" Hinego said hotly.

Asdelar laughed. "You could have fooled me."

Hinego had been gripping Asdelar's shoulder with his free hand, and his fingers clenched abruptly, his already unfocused gaze wavering. An unpleasant expression crossed his face. "Stop," he gasped. "Stop spinning, or I'll be sick all over you."

Asdelar took another turn or two, then reluctantly came to a stop. He took a few wavering steps, but Hinego's balance was even more thrown off, and he staggered uncontrollably in the direction of the door.

Asdelar waited until he was sure which way was up and which was down before hurrying after him. He clapped a hand on his shoulder, jerking him to a halt. "Whoa, there, are you really going to be sick, or are you just trying to sneak off?"

Hinego gritted his teeth, trying to pull free. "I can be sick in the alley, or I can be sick right here on your boots. Your choice, Blade."

"All right all right, wait a moment." Asdelar turned and tried to pick Morasa out of the crowd, squinting in a failed attempt to focus. He didn't realize he was teetering back and forth until Hinego's hand latched onto his arm to hold him still.

Finally he spotted the older woman cozying up to a flirtatious young girl at a table by the wall. Asdelar was vaguely surprised. He'd half expected her to follow Hinego to his room at the end of the night. "Looks like Morasa's occupied at the moment," he noted, but he was talking to thin air. He looked around in confusion, then stumbled out into the blissfully cool night air.

He caught a glimpse of Hinego ducking into the side alley and followed. He stopped at the alleyway's opening, leaning heavily against the wall and politely looking away as Hinego put a hand to the wall and emptied the contents of his churning stomach onto the already filthy ground.

"No shame in it," he advised, staring up at the stars with drunken contentment. "Vomiting usually makes me feel better when I've had too much to drink."

Hinego pushed himself away from the wall, wiping a shaking hand across his mouth. He shot Asdelar a venomous look. "I cannot believe I let you idiots talk me into that," he growled, spitting distastefully to the side. He stumbled a bit, found his balance, and strode out of the alley angrily.

Asdelar laughed, trying to catch his arm as he went by. "Oh come on, Hinego, don't be like that."

Hinego evaded his grasp. "I'm going back to the Cove," he snapped. "The night air will help clear my head. If you find some tramp and actually manage to sneak her in, attempt to keep it down. I swear I'll kill you in your sleep if you keep me awake with all the noise."

Asdelar made another hasty grab, seizing him by the elbow. "Now hold on a minute," he said, offended. "I came out to enjoy myself. Looking for a bedmate was not my intention. I'm getting a little sick of you practically referring to me as a whore."

Hinego wrenched his arm free. "You don't argue too strenuously against your reputation. And it's no business of mine, so long as it doesn't interfere with my sleeping schedule."

Asdelar opened his mouth for an angry retort, and that was when the attack came.

He was drunker than he'd thought; he didn't see the man who came rushing at him out of the dark until too late, and there was no time to block the blow that cracked across his jaw. He reeled from the hit, lost his footing, and fell in a rather ungraceful heap, spitting curses.

Two other shadowy figures appeared as if out of thin air, and the moonlight cast dull light off of the edges of the knives in their hands. They didn't speak, but spread out around Hinego, since Asdelar was finding it impossible to collect himself enough to get to his feet.

Hinego held himself poised for battle, fists up defensively to block any blows aimed at his face. His narrowed eyes flickered around at the three men, sizing them up. "Assaulting a Red? Not very bright," he warned. "Assuming you get out of this alive, you could be hanged for such a crime."

One of the men, bolder than his companions, rushed at Hinego, knife lifted for a fatal blow.

Asdelar's heart leapt into his throat, but Hinego was already reacting to the threat.

Hinego was smaller than his attacker, but it didn't seem to give him any pause. He dodged the first swipe of the blade nimbly, then his fist was darting out quick as thought— *Crack!* His assailant's head snapped back as the blow landed squarely on his nose. Without pausing Hinego dropped low and swung his leg in a chopping motion low to the ground, sweeping the other man's legs out from under him and bringing him to the ground.

The next man jumped in, hoping to catch him off guard, but Hinego was ready for him. From his position on the ground he used his arms to lift his body, already kicking up over his head. His foot connected solidly with the side of the man's head and sent him crashing into the wall. Hinego twisted fluidly, and the overhead kick became a flip that put him on his feet again just in time to clap both hands over the wrist of the third man, effectively halting the path of his knife. Wrapping his fingers around the trapped wrist, he wrenched the man's hand ruthlessly.

With a cry of pain, the man released the knife. Before it had even hit the ground Hinego jerked the man in close and dealt him a resounding head-butt. The attacker howled, staggering back, and Hinego released him, blinking rapidly to clear his vision. It only took him a moment to steady himself.

Before his opponent could think to defend himself, Hinego slammed a fist into his throat, practically crushing it. The man crumpled to the ground, wheezing desperately.

It all happened in a shockingly short amount of time, all of it almost too quick for Asdelar to keep up with in his inebriated state. He sat frozen on the ground, mouth open as he stared in something like awe at Hinego.

Hinego backed away from his defeated assailants, bouncing lightly on the balls of his feet and readying himself for another rush.

The mysterious attackers, however, had had enough. They scrambled to their feet and limped off as quickly as they could.

He snarled a curse and took off after them.

"Hey, wait!" Asdelar forced himself to get up and staggered after him. The blow to his jaw had cleared his head a bit, and he raced to catch up.

He didn't have far to go. Hinego stood tensely in the middle of the street half a block from the pub, looking around in visible frustration. "Where the hell did they go?" he snapped, fists clenched as he looked right and left, eyes blazing. "Slippery bastards."

Asdelar panted for breath, squinting in the darkness. "They might have dodged down another alley," he suggested. "Or gone inside somewhere." He blew out a loud sigh, reaching up absently to touch the side of his jaw. "Damn. Pretty determined for pick-pockets."

"They weren't robbers," Hinego growled. "They didn't make any threats or demands, and none of them attempted to relieve you of your purse while you were on the ground." He let loose a stream of impressive oaths. "Damn it all, they were waiting for us specifically. Someone must have overheard us outside of Sheidach's. There's no other explanation."

Asdelar's eyebrows shot up. "Good grief, are you sure? That would mean—"

"That means Lady Valera didn't run away, or if she did, she was snatched up soon afterward," Hinego said grimly. "And the rope at the ford was a clue, after all. All we need are the details: are these the men responsible, and does that mean the Duke's daughter is still here? Or were they left here to deal with anyone who might be following?"

Asdelar took a deep breath, raking his hair out of his eyes. "Well, we aren't going to figure anything out standing around out here. Besides, I'm still a bit too drunk to think logically. Let's go get Morasa and head back to the Cove. We'll need her help anyway. If there's another explanation for the attack, she might know. Maybe there are people in town who have a grudge against the Imalt-wor."

"Maybe." But Hinego didn't sound convinced.

"By the way, you handled yourself very well back

there," Asdelar complimented as they turned and made their way back to the pub. "I don't think I'll ever question the ability of an unarmed Red again. You probably saved my hide. I'm not really in any condition to deal with three thugs tonight."

Hinego snorted quietly.

"No, really. It was quite an impressive show of skill. You're quite a sight in battle." Asdelar grinned, throwing his arm around Hinego's shoulders. "Now that I've seen you in action, that's another step in that ... what is it called, Fa-wor. Perhaps we can learn to fight side by side after all."

"Faew-bor," Hinego corrected, trying to shrug him off.

"Whatever. We'll make a fearsome team, you and I."

"We shall see."

"Quit trying to wriggle away, there's a good man. I don't particularly trust myself to walk in a straight line just yet."

Chapter Seven

"I can't take you anywhere," Morasa grumbled without looking up from what she was doing. "I swear, Idra, you attract trouble like the plague."

Asdelar winced as she dabbed a bit forcefully with a damp cloth at a scrape on his arm. "It's just a scratch," he insisted. "I can take care of it."

She ignored him. She was quietly fuming, probably upset that she'd been dragged away from her dark corner at the pub. The woman she'd been forced to leave behind had looked decidedly put-out as well. "You couldn't even spend one night brawl-free, could you? Do you go hunting down fights when you're irritable, or do you exude some scent that lowlifes can sniff out and use to track you down?"

"Stop your nagging, Morasa," Hinego snapped from where he was standing tensely by the window, gazing out at the dark streets. "Those men had something to do with Lady Valera's disappearance, I'm sure of it."

"Oh, okay, then. You're sure. That must mean it's true." She tossed the rag aside and got to her feet, placing her hands on her hips and glaring at him. "What possible proof do you have, Hinego? For all you know they were just pickpockets! You two presented an easy target, and they took their chances. My squad will ferret them out in the morning."

"I'm telling you, this was not some botched attempt at theft," Hinego retorted. "This was different."

"How? *How* was it different?" She sighed, scratching roughly at her scalp. "Never mind. We'll know after we've caught them. We'll question them thoroughly."

"If they had something to do with Lady Valera's disappearance, it's unlikely they'll stick around for your interrogation," Hinego pointed out. "They'll be gone by morning."

Morasa threw her arms up in disgust. "You're impossible! Hinego, listen to yourself! All you have to go on is a broken rope and a hunch! This mission of yours is making you a bit paranoid, if you ask me."

"I *didn't* ask you."

Asdelar cleared his throat to get their attention. "If you two are finished arguing like a married couple, I'd like to point out how late it's getting. If we still expect to have a somewhat early start in the morning, we should get some sleep soon."

Morasa spun on her heel to gaze sternly down at him. "And you." She smiled suddenly. "I like you. It's almost a pity that you're stuck with ..." she jerked her thumb over her shoulder, indicating her scowling friend, "old grumpy guts here. Don't let him get you into too much trouble, you hear me? And try not to take anything he says too personally. I think underneath it all he's just a big softy."

"Weren't you leaving?" Hinego said a bit snidely.

She made a face at him.

Asdelar rose to walk her to the door. "You won't be seeing us off in the morning?"

"I doubt it. I'll probably still be asleep when you leave. If not, I'll be looking for those men who accosted you." She clucked her tongue in sympathy, reaching up to lightly touch his bruised jaw. "He sure got you good. Make sure you keep a cool cloth on that, or it's going to puff up something nasty." She wiggled her fingers at them in farewell. "Well, good luck with your silly quest, boys. Make sure you look me up on your way back home."

"Women," Hinego muttered as soon as the door shut behind her. "Is nagging all they're good at?"

Asdelar couldn't help but smile. There had been no real scorn to Hinego's voice. "They're good for lots of things."

"Don't start."

Asdelar chuckled, moving over to stand beside him and peek out at the empty streets. "Don't be cruel, Hinego. It's easy to see you care about one another. She's a good woman. And something tells me it would be dangerous to be on her bad side."

Hinego snorted but didn't respond.

Asdelar grew more serious, rubbing carefully at the lump on his jaw. "She has a point. There's no way of knowing if those men had anything to do with the Duke's daughter. Do you think we should stay here another day and wait until she's finished interrogating them?"

"If she finds them, you mean," Hinego said. "No, we can't waste time here. She can always send a message if she finds out anything useful. We must be catching up, and staying here another day would just further increase the distance between us and them."

"You're so sure this is a kidnapping, then?"

Hinego shook his head briefly. "I can't say for

sure," he admitted grudgingly. "But it sure seems that way. I'd rather be proven wrong then find out I'm right when it's too late to do anything about it."

Asdelar shrugged. "If you say so." He reached up and flicked aside Hinego's dark bangs, pressing his fingertips lightly to his brow.

Hinego jerked back, glaring at him suspiciously. "What are you doing?"

"Just seeing if you'd given yourself a knot when you head-butted that man. This just proves your head really is as hard as a rock." A slow grin spread his lips. "I never knew the fighting style of the Imalt-wor could be so fluid and effective. I've seen dancers with worse grace. And you weren't even sober."

If he'd hoped to fluster Hinego with flattery, he was disappointed. Hinego frowned at him. "You're comparing fighting to dancing?"

Asdelar laughed. "It's not an insult, trust me. Do you think you could show me some of it sometime? It might come in handy if I ever find myself without a sword."

Hinego arched a brow. "You? I don't think so."

"Oh come on, why not?"

He turned away as if bored of the conversation. "Go to bed, Blade. It's late."

Asdelar turned and strode over to the bed, stretching himself out comfortably.

Hinego watched him blankly. "What do you think you're doing?"

"Going to bed, obviously." He punched the pillow a few times to plump it up, then settled back down again as if he belonged there.

"That's my bed, you idiot. Go to your own room."

"By the way, I thought I told you to stop calling me

Blade."

Hinego's lip curled slightly in an impatient sneer. "I'm not in the mood for your stupid games. It's late, and I'm tired. Now get off that bed this instant."

Asdelar laced his fingers behind his head and offered his most insulting grin. "Make me."

"*Make me*?" Hinego repeated. He stomped over and pointed imperiously towards the door. "Get out of my room before I throw you out, you immature, immoral, lazy sack of—" His tirade ended in what could only be described as a startled yelp as a hand snagged him by the front of his shirt and dragged him down.

He managed to brace himself against the side of the bed with his knees, bent over at an uncomfortable angle. A moment later Asdelar propped himself up with his free hand, raising himself into a sitting position so that they were inches apart. He kept his grip on Hinego's shirt and refused to let go, his eyes dancing with mirth.

"It's a big bed. We can share."

He struggled to pry Asdelar's hand from his shirt, his ears red despite the note of incredulous affront in his voice. "Let go of me, you lummox! Do you want me to break your arm?"

"So which is it, Hinego?" Asdelar asked abruptly, gaze intent. "You're an impossible man to decipher. I'd assumed you prefer women because of how you treat me, but it's obvious it embarrasses you in a not-so-unpleasant way when I tease you. You certainly don't seem interested in Morasa, and she's quite a good-looking woman. Trying to figure you out is making my head hurt, so why don't you just save me the trouble and lay it all out for me?"

Hinego gaped at him in disbelief. "What—you want to talk about that *now*? After what happened with those men? Are you insane?" He tried to pull away. "What business is it of yours, you impertinent oaf?"

"Perhaps now's not the best time," Asdelar agreed, though he sounded amused. He released him and got to his feet when Hinego dodged out of reach. "All right, be the man of mystery all you like. I'll figure it out eventually—one way or another."

"What is that supposed to mean?" Hinego demanded warily.

"Never you mind." Asdelar grinned and headed for the door. "Sweet dreams, Hinego."

He was gone before Hinego could gather his scattered wits enough to come up with a suitably scathing retort.

~~*

The following morning Asdelar's head ached and his stomach twisted unpleasantly at the prospect of breakfast; but he had suffered worse hangovers and was able to ride with little difficulty. Morasa had disappeared into town with the rest of her squad in search of the bandits from the previous night. Asdelar regretted being unable to say a proper farewell, but they couldn't afford to wait around for her return. He was feeling better within an hour, the breeze on his face and the earthy scent in the air helping bring him around.

It was Hinego who was in bad shape. He had practically dragged himself onto his saddle, and sat slumped and miserable for the first several hours as they made their way slowly out of town and down the dusty southern road.

Asdelar managed to coax some bread and water down him, then prudently left him to his own devices for the rest of the morning. If anything, Hinego's temper was even shorter and more ferocious when he was feeling under the weather.

By noon he seemed to be doing better. He sat up straight in his saddle, looked around with sharp eyes, and even ate a bit more bread. But any hesitant attempts on Asdelar's part at starting a conversation were quickly shot down. Pouting at the return of the cold shoulder routine, Asdelar eventually gave up. The longer the silence between them grew, the tenser both men felt, until Asdelar began to feel slightly paranoid. He stared at Hinego's back, chewing nervously on a hangnail and working himself into a private tizzy. He was unused to having such difficulty making friends. Hinego's constant rebuffs were finally getting to him.

Had he gone too far, teasing Hinego the previous night? If Hinego had no interest in men, he might be even more uncomfortable in Asdelar's company now. Or perhaps he was still angry about getting drunk. *And I was pretty useless when those cutthroats showed up,* Asdelar thought with a wince. *Maybe he thinks I really am just a big burden. Maybe he can't stand to even look at me.*

Asdelar's inner pity party probably would have gone on for quite some time if Hinego hadn't turned abruptly in his saddle to offer him an impatient glare late in the afternoon.

"What are you doing hanging back like a whipped dog?" he snapped. "I am not going to give myself whiplash trying to hold a conversation with you."

Pleased and a bit surprised, Asdelar nudged his horse up alongside Hinego's mare. "I apologize," he said quickly, wanting to clear the air. "If I was a bit too, er, forward last night, I mean. I was only teasing. And I won't make you drink so much again in the future if—"

"I'm a grown man, I can think for myself," Hinego cut him off a bit huffily. "Nobody forced me to drink that much ale. It was my own stupidity at fault." His dark eyes flashed Asdelar a sideways, begrudging look, and everything was all right again.

Encouraged by the reluctant peace offering, Asdelar attempted to steer him into a civilized conversation when they stopped by the roadside to stretch their legs and eat a quick lunch.

"So what made you decide to try out for the Imalt-wor?" he asked a bit hesitantly, very much aware of how touchy Hinego was about discussing his personal life. "Was it a family tradition or something?"

Hinego didn't favor him with a glance, eyes tracking the sky in search of his hawk, but Asdelar took it as a good sign that he answered at all. "In a way. My grandfather was a Red, and I always looked up to him and liked to listen to his campaign stories. As soon as he realized how serious I was about it, he made sure I got the proper training. I tried out when I was seventeen, then again when I was eighteen, and I made the cut that time." He hesitated, flicking Asdelar a glance. "I suppose you're the same?" he finally asked, the question a bit forced, as if he was only carrying on the conversation to appease Asdelar. "Following in the footsteps of your father or some such thing?"

"Oh, no." Asdelar flicked away a hard crust and nibbled thoughtfully on the softer middle of the bread. "I never knew my father. But I'd heard about the Blades, and it sounded like a grand life. I had the blacksmith make me a crude sword when I was about thirteen, and used to practice secretly. My mother would have boxed my ears if she'd known. Peasants' sons aren't exactly allowed to carry weapons, even dull ones. My mother did some tailoring for a minor nobleman, and his son would do mock duels with me sometimes in the woods. He was kind of my first teacher. Turns out I had a knack for the sword. After that I attended every tourney I could sneak into. As a spectator, of course, to see how it was really done."

"Tourney?"

"I'm not sure how the Imalt-wor do things, but the Banam-hin hold yearly tournaments to find the cream of the crop for their ranks. It's also a way for them to pick out those with potential so they know to keep an eye on them later down the road. The tournaments are open to the public; the money from the proceedings goes to new training gear."

"I thought the crown paid for all the Gravemen's needs," Hinego said with a touch of surprise.

"For the most part, yes. Taxes take care of our barracks and armor, but we are expected to take care of the rest ourselves: training equipment and trips to the blacksmith to fix a broken sword, for example."

Hinego rubbed an apple against his sleeve distractedly, eyes drifting as he remembered his own acceptance into the Gravemen. "We have a competition, as well," he said after a moment. "Though it is a very private affair that takes place indoors, in an enclosed arena. The only ones who can view the fighting matches are those who already have the red sash. Squad leaders sometimes lay claim to new recruits there, if they are short a man." He arched a brow. "So one day you decided to compete? Who did you find to train you before you entered this tournament? Surely not the noble's son."

Asdelar gave a sheepish laugh. "I didn't know who to ask," he admitted. "I grew up in a small village not far from the city; I knew no Blades personally, much less anyone who was trained even in the basics of sword fighting. My mother no longer tailored for that nobleman, so I didn't see the son anymore. I thought I would give it a go anyhow. I entered the tournament when I was nineteen, and ..." He shrugged self-consciously, taking a sip from his canteen.

Hinego stared at him in mounting disbelief. "Surely they didn't accept you?"

"Well ... not right away," Asdelar hedged. "I wasn't taken in as a full Banam-hin. But one of the sergeants thought I had a lot of raw potential for someone without any formal training, so he arranged for me to move into the barracks and took over my training himself. It's not an unusual occurrence; there were three other trainees besides myself from earlier tournaments."

Hinego's brow furrowed suspiciously. "How old are you?" he demanded.

Asdelar grinned. "How old do I look?"

Hinego scowled openly. "Enough of your teasing, Blade. Just answer the question."

Asdelar mumbled something into the mouth of his canteen.

"What's that? Speak up."

Asdelar lowered the canteen reluctantly. "I'll be two and twenty in a few months' time."

Hinego gaped. "Are you telling me you've had less than three years' worth of official training with a sword and you're a Blade?"

Asdelar shrugged again, looking uncomfortable. "You don't have to act like it's anything special. Aren't you a bit young for an Imalt-wor?"

Hinego bristled slightly, then shook his head sharply. "I'm only a year younger than you, Blade. But I've had official training since I was a boy. I showed an aptitude for it; it's why I was accepted at such a young age. I've heard of Blades who have spent their entire lives training with the sword, yet you're telling me you were accepted without having ever had a proper teacher and that it took only a few years to make you worthy of that armor." His gaze went meaningfully to the saddlebags where Asdelar's ceremonial armor was stashed.

Asdelar offered him a cool look. "There's no reason for me to lie about this," he said. "I wouldn't—"

"I'm not calling you a liar," Hinego cut him off, studying him keenly. "It just seems that perhaps there is more to you than I first assumed."

Asdelar's face broke into a bright smile.

"Don't go getting any foolish notions in that head of yours," Hinego grumbled, seeming embarrassed at Asdelar's pleasure. He got to his feet hastily. "Finish your meal, Blade. We'd best get back on our way. The Crossroads is just a few miles from here, and we can try to ferret out more information there."

Even Asdelar, with his limited knowledge of the countryside, had heard of the Crossroads.

The King's Road, which they were currently on, was the oldest and most traveled road in Predala, being the one straight shot to the capital city of Oneth. It stretched from north to south, cutting through many towns and offering itself as the preferred route of merchants as well as anyone else intent on getting to the city. It was also patrolled at regular intervals by the Imalt-wor, and though there were not nearly enough of them to cover the entire length of the road, one never knew when a squad could be found traveling a particular stretch. The threat of their presence was enough to keep the majority of the road bandits at bay, especially during the day.

The only other road that could rival the King's Road in length and usefulness was what had commonly become known as the Farmer's Way, a wider road that led from east to west, beaten into the grasslands by countless wagons over the years. This was the road used by farmers with goods to sell, as well as simple travelers moving from one place to the other.

The Crossroads was where these two roads met, but this was as far as Asdelar's knowledge on the subject went.

He took out his map once he was in the saddle, quickly finding the Crossroads marked on the map. "How do we get information at the Crossroads?" he asked dubiously. "I've never heard of there being any towns or villages set up so close to it."

"There aren't," Hinego said. "If my memory serves me correctly, there is a village a few miles away from the Crossroads, but that isn't what I meant. We are going to get information from the people who are always at the Crossroads, whether they're supposed to be there or not. Gods know the Imalt-wor have tried again and again to get them to clear off. They're like weeds; they always come back when no one's looking. We've never tried too strenuously to get them to leave. They tend to only stay for a few months at a time anyhow, and they're always cycling out, so there's always new people from all over the country. That means information, which is valuable. We'll look the other way as long as they don't cause any trouble, and they in turn are usually fairly cooperative with us."

"Who exactly are you talking about?" Asdelar exclaimed.

Hinego cast him a slightly impatient look. "The Rovers, you oaf. Don't tell me you've never heard of *them*."

He had. Asdelar unconsciously wrapped his fingers tightly around the hilt of his sword, struggling with a warring sense of unease and curiosity. "Are they as bad as everyone says?"

Hinego nodded, eyes forward but face grim. "Just because the Imalt-wor need them for information doesn't mean we trust them. But if this really is a kidnapping and Lady Valera's gone this way, they'll know about it."

"What if they're behind the kidnapping?" Asdelar asked pointedly.

"The thought had crossed my mind." A cold smile twitched at Hinego's mouth. "If that's the case, then perhaps you'll get the opportunity to show off the skills that got you into the ranks of the Banam-hin so quickly."

Chapter Eight

The Rovers were at the Crossroads, just as Hinego had predicted.

Asdelar, who had seen only a handful of them in the city, could do nothing but gape as Hinego led him to the cluster of wagons and brightly-colored tents laid out boldly in the grass just off of the intersection of the two roads.

Officially the Rovers were nothing more than homeless nomads, traveling the roads when and how they pleased, going from town to town to hawk their wares and put down temporary roots until they were inevitably driven out or, in rarer circumstances, simply felt the urge to move on. They were also notorious thieves and brawlers, and seemed to have a knack for getting into trouble wherever they went.

They were viewed as an unwelcome pest by just about everybody and were usually forced to set up camp outside town limits or risk being lynched.

Despite this, every boy and girl wished secretly, but fervently to be a little Rover child: to dance for money, travel the countryside, and lead a life of frivolity and mischief. It was an appealing life to youngsters who did not know the darker sides of things.

"If there's coin missing, a fight started, or a man cheated, a Rover's passed through," Hinego muttered, the old saying coming unbidden to his lips at the sight of the rowdy bunch.

Asdelar shot him a sharp look, but didn't have a chance to respond. At their approach, it seemed as if every Rover in the small caravan had come out of their tents and wagons and were now collecting themselves along the side of the road, all of them smiling.

Asdelar's hand fell to the hilt of his sword automatically, but he resisted the impulse to draw it. He told himself sternly not to let the rumors he'd heard color his first impression of the people. Hinego gave him a look that clearly said 'keep your mouth shut', and reined in his mare once they'd gotten close enough to converse with the band without shouting.

One of them, a large woman with a colorful scarf tied over her dark hair, pushed her way through the crowd and offered an elaborate bow, flashing yellowed teeth as she smiled ingratiatingly up at the mounted men. She was covered in jewelry, none of it matching, and the uncountable bracelets, earrings, and necklaces jangled every time she moved. "Good day to you, fine gentlemen. I be Rinara, the Matriarch of this sorry lot. Do you care to look over what poor wares we have to offer?"

"Actually, we would like to ask you a few questions," Hinego said, back straight as he gazed down at her with a carefully neutral expression.

Rinara's quick eyes had already noticed the man's

tell-tale red sash. "Me 'n' mine just got here last moon," she assured him, trying another smile. "We've broken no laws here, Imalt-wor."

"This has nothing to do with your tribe," Hinego assured her, opening his hand to show her the three coins he held in his palm. "I am merely seeking information."

Rinara shuffled a bit closer, eyeing the coins greedily. "The Rovers are always willin' to tell what they know," she said quickly. "And of course the Imalt-wor have our full cooperation anytime they ask it."

Hinego nodded, closing his fist over the money again. "We're looking for a young girl, around sixteen—"

"Seventeen," Asdelar murmured.

"Seventeen years of age." Hinego's eyes swept the group. "She may have been alone, but it's more likely she would be in the company of some men. Perhaps unwillingly."

"Many girls come through the Crossroads, good sir," Rinara hedged. "Could you not be a bit more descriptive of the lady?"

Hinego hesitated, glancing towards Asdelar. He had never personally met the Duke's daughter, but she was known to visit the King on occasion.

"She's a bit small for her age," Asdelar spoke up, lowering his hand to just above his horse's shoulder. "About this tall, slender, with very long red hair. If she spoke at all, she might have seemed kind of high and prim, even a bit rude, perhaps."

There was a smattering of amused laughter from the Rovers, and Rinara's smile broadened a bit. "You seem an honest, blunt sort of man," she noted, eyeing Asdelar up and down. She glanced at each of them shrewdly, then turned to address those gathered behind her in a ringing voice. "Well, speak up, you lot. Anybody notice a girl by that description passing through here lately?"

There were head shakes and thoughtful frowns, but the overall consensus seemed to be in the negative. Rinara turned back to Asdelar and Hinego and spread her arms wide, offering another gap-toothed smile. "Well, there you have it." She held up a finger as if a thought had just occurred to her. "This here ent everyone, you know. There's some that still be inside. If you but give me a moment, I'll go ask around." She indicated some of the tents which had their walls rolled up, open for business. "Why not take a look about, see if we have something that catches your fancy? Mayhap naught so fine as what two gentlemen such as yourselves are used to, but there are sometimes surprisin' treasures to be found."

Hinego looked ready to turn down the offer, but Asdelar was itching with eagerness to check out an actual Rover caravan. He'd been expecting hostility or men armed to the teeth, but so far the Rovers seemed quite friendly. "We can only spare a few minutes," he said, getting down from his horse and ignoring Hinego's glare.

Rinara flashed him another wide smile and hurried over to the covered wagons to speak to those who had not come out yet.

Hinego reluctantly got down from his mare, but didn't relinquish the reins right away. "Lorem, you imbecile," he hissed, "what do you think you're doing? We don't have time to consort with these—"

"I just want to look. Relax." Asdelar dodged past the welcoming crowd before he could protest. Hinego muttered to himself under his breath, then hastily tied up their horses on the picket alongside the Rovers' mules. Chin held high, he strode after Asdelar.

There were nearly a dozen open tents, the odds and ends of the Rovers' trade spread out on blankets for perusal underneath each canvas awning.

Hinego felt his lip curl involuntarily as he glanced over the first tent's offerings. Junk. Useless baubles and trash, none of it worth paying for as far as he was concerned. He had in his time run across an interesting knick-knack or two in a Rover's tent, but the fare before him looked like the usual oddities that only the gullible or very young would be interested in. Surely Asdelar would lose interest once he realized this.

"Hinego, look at this! I've never seen one of these before! Oh, look, I had one of these when I was a boy ..."

Hinego lifted his gaze skyward in a silent prayer for patience. "Why am I not surprised at your fascination with this ..." he caught the vendor looking at him and finished lamely, "stuff?"

The man in charge of the tent immediately seized on his potential customer, ignoring Hinego and his obvious disdain for the goods. The old man had very few teeth left in his head, but displayed all four of them in an encouraging smile as he lifted this and that for Asdelar's inspection. "This here is a good luck charm; you wear it around your neck underneath your clothes and good fortune will follow you in your footsteps. Very hard to procure, these are. We make 'em ourselves, but we sell very few. And I'll bet you've never seen one of these before. It's called a Truth Looker. Look into this and you will see the truths inside yourself."

"It's just a pocket mirror," Hinego said in disgust.

The seller acted as if he hadn't even spoken, holding out a length of gauzy material. "This is the finest lace, spun by the women of the western towns. Feel that? You won't find anything so fine down in the south. It makes a perfect gift for a lovely lady."

Despite Hinego's protests, Asdelar ended up purchasing the good luck charm for what seemed to Hinego a ridiculous amount of money for a simple carved rock on a leather thong. He then proceeded to go from tent to tent, with Hinego trailing unwillingly after him.

"You're like a child," Hinego huffed, amused despite himself at Asdelar's simple delight over a pretty little colored glass vial. "This is all junk and you know it. They certainly don't sell this garbage in Oneth."

"Which is why it's so fascinating," Asdelar retorted, carefully easing the top off the delicate vial and giving the contents a quick sniff.

Hinego made a noncommittal noise in his throat, using his fingers to sift through the collection of jarred and bottled 'remedies' and 'medicines' spread out. "It's gullible people like you who encourage these charlatans," he muttered, just low enough to keep the woman from overhearing. "None of this does what it's advertised to do. Wart balm? Love potion? They can't be serious."

"You are no fun whatsoever," Asdelar declared, and Hinego watched in resignation as money exchanged hands and the pretty vial disappeared into

Asdelar's pocket. "I'll bet you're a horrible date. Where do you take women for a good time? The city hall of records?"

Hinego crossed his arms over his chest, scowling as he looked around suspiciously. "I am not getting into this with you. Where is the Matriarch? She's certainly taking her time." He made a face at Asdelar's back as he stepped over to the next tent. "She's probably waiting until you spend every coin you have out here."

"Oh, hush."

A lot of the Rovers had returned to their wagons or fires, casting the occasional glance towards their guests, but otherwise leaving both men to themselves. When one of them strode boldly over, Hinego tensed, not sure what to expect.

"I see you're enjoying our wares," the man noted with a quick smile as he sidled up next to Asdelar, glancing from the goods to his face. "We sure do appreciate your business." His eyes flickered to the sword at Asdelar's waist. "I have to say, it's rare that gennelmen like yourself come buyin' from our kind. They usually turn up their noses at us, they do." He didn't look at Hinego when he said this, but it was obvious whom he was referring to.

Asdelar laughed lightly, idly rolling a tin thimble in between his thumb and forefinger as he met the other man's bold stare. "I don't get to travel much," he admitted. "I've never seen such an interesting array of goods. They may not be very valuable, but I admit I have a slight weakness for odds and ends. Who knows when I may ever see some of these things again?"

Hinego stared at his partner. Either he was

reading too much into things, or ...

Was the idiot *flirting*?

No, surely not. Asdelar was simply being polite.

The Rover smiled, spreading his arms to indicate the tents. "Nowhere else will you find such a selection," he boasted. "We admit most of this is of little value, as you say. But everything has a use. One man's trash is another's treasure, that's our motto."

Hinego stepped up beside Asdelar, eyeing the young man with a slight frown. "I thought your motto was 'Get them before they get you'," he corrected blandly, studying the friendly Rover a bit more thoroughly. He was tall like Asdelar, if not as broad-shouldered, and could not have been more than a few years older than either of them. He was as tanned as Hinego, but his hair was a rich brown and in need of a barber; the wind-tossed curls hung over his forehead, covered his ears, and were nearly as long as Asdelar's straight tresses. But where Asdelar's fairer locks were professionally cut and stylish, brushing the tops of his shoulders, this man looked as if he had simply neglected to take a knife to the mess in months. He didn't seem to be missing any teeth, and he seemed handsome and friendly enough.

Hinego disliked him on sight.

"I see you've had some dealings with our people before," the man noted with a sardonic smile. "But then, the Imalt-wor have often crossed paths with our kind. Not always in a cordial manner, might I add."

Asdelar cut in smoothly, perhaps trying to forestall a confrontation. "I don't believe I caught your name." He extended his hand courteously. "Asdelar Lorem."

The man had dimples. *Dimples*, for gods' sakes. He grasped Asdelar's hand in a warm handshake. "A pleasure to meet you, Sir Lorem." For the first time Hinego became acutely aware of the Rover accent that gave the man's words a strange, rich twist. "Fikin's me name. Fikin Abaastor."

"Oh, please, none of this 'Sir Lorem' nonsense," Asdelar laughed. "'Asdelar' is just fine. I'm ..." he cut himself off before he could admit to his lack of nobility, but managed to finish somewhat casually, "not of any great stature anyhow."

If Fikin noticed the verbal stumble, he gave no sign of it. Neither had he released Asdelar's hand, Hinego noticed with an inner eye roll. "I wonder if you'd sit with some of us for a spell." Fikin indicated a small group of men sitting around one of the fires, laughing together and passing around a flask. "We're always eager to hear news and stories from trav'lers."

Asdelar smiled, but Hinego was having none of that foolishness. "I'm afraid we cannot dawdle," he said stiffly. "We have already stayed longer than we intended. Time is not on our side, and we must continue on our way."

Fikin finally relinquished Asdelar's hand. "Of course. I understand. Headin' south, are ya? Searchin' for the girl?"

"Yes," Asdelar answered before Hinego could silence him.

Fikin glanced at each of them in turn. "I suppose you'll continue on to Nehalm? Providin' you don't find this myst'ry girl before then, I mean."

"Yes, that's right. We'll be making a few stops along the way, of course. In ..." Asdelar paused, thinking, "Pran and Belor, first."

Hinego clenched his teeth. Of all the times for the buffoon to show off his new map reading skills. He tried to remind himself that it was ignorance of the outside world and not stupidity that ailed his partner.

Fikin looked inordinately pleased at the confirmation. "Splendid. I don't suppose I could ask a boon of you?" He hurried on when Hinego opened his mouth to protest. "I have business in Nehalm, y'see, but the caravan's headin' a bit more east. Since we're headin' the same way, mebbe I could travel with you for part of the way? Just until we reach Nehalm, of course. Travelin's always better when you've got companions, I always say."

"Absolutely not," Hinego said.

"Excuse us a moment," Asdelar murmured. Taking Hinego firmly by the elbow, he pulled him aside, just out of hearing range. "Hinego," he whispered in reproach, "why in the gods' names are you being so rude to the man? He's been nothing but courteous to us."

Hinego wrenched his arm free indignantly, glaring up at him. "Don't be daft," he hissed. "We are on official business! We can't have that thief tagging along. Not only would he get in the way and ask awkward questions, but he can't be trusted. He could rob us blind or cut our throats in the night! Or both, if I know Rovers."

Asdelar frowned. "That's unfair. I'm disappointed in you, Hinego. These people have been friendly to us, but you're letting your prejudices get in the way. If Fikin does start asking questions, there's nothing that says we must answer. And what fool would rob one of the Imalt-wor? Especially one so obviously itching for a fight."

"And what happens the next time we're jumped by armed men in a dark alley?" Hinego snapped.

"From what I've heard, Rovers can take care of themselves," Asdelar said patiently. "Even I can see they carry knives, though they've been trying to keep them out of sight with a Red around. Come on, Hinego. You aren't the most talkative fellow, and it will be nice to have someone to exchange stories with on the trip. He's friendly and forthright. If it makes you feel better, I promise to take full responsibility for him."

Hinego drew in a deep breath through his nose, reining in his temper. A part of him knew that it would be a bad idea to have a tag-along on their mission, but the other part of him was already giving in. Asdelar had promised to keep an eye on him—and at least he had noticed the knives, so he was not completely oblivious—and it was only for a few days. He could argue about it until he eventually won, but he could see already by the determined set of Asdelar's jaw that it would be a long argument, and they had wasted enough time already.

"Fine," he growled, jabbing a finger forcefully in Asdelar's chest. "But you had better watch him close, Lorem. The second he puts a toe out of line, he's gone. Do you hear me?"

Asdelar smiled brilliantly. "Right. I understand. Don't worry so much, Hinego." He turned back to Fikin, raising his voice to be heard. "You can come with us as far as Nehalm," he said cheerfully. "Will you be ready to leave soon? My friend here is a bit impatient to get on the move again."

Fikin nodded eagerly, already turning away. "My thanks, lords. I'll be right back. I'll go and check in on

Missus Rinara as well."

"A Blade and a Red traveling with a Rover," Hinego muttered sourly, crossing his arms over his chest and scowling at Fikin's retreating back. "If Morasa could see this, she would laugh herself sick."

"Oh, relax, Hinego," Asdelar scoffed, giving him a playful push and earning a dark look in return. "It's one man against two Gravemen! What's the worst that could happen?"

Hinego's expression turned pained. "I really wish you hadn't said that."

Chapter Nine

Hinego had not been expecting to get any proper information for his money, but Rinara surprised them when she returned from the wagons.

One of the Rovers she had questioned admitted to seeing a girl pass by in the company of a handful of men not two weeks before.

"He says she wore a cloak and hood and that the group rode on late at night without stopping," Rinara reported. "If she were a redhead, it were impossible to make out."

It could have been coincidence, but there was a slim chance that the two Gravemen had at last had an actual sighting of the missing noblewoman. Hinego gave her the three coins he'd promised, and they were on their way once again, this time with a new companion.

The Rovers had no horses, only hardy mules that were used exclusively to pull the low-slung wagons. This meant that Fikin had no choice but to hitch a ride with one of them. Asdelar graciously—and a bit predictably, Hinego thought—offered to share his own saddle.

Hinego grumbled under his breath about how the added burden meant more rests for the horse and watched the two men distrustfully as they rode ahead. He refused to have a Rover at his back out of sight and had insisted they take the lead. Fikin knew the way, and from the rear Hinego could keep a sharp eye on the man.

Fikin rode behind Asdelar, arms wound loosely but comfortably around his waist for balance as he chattered about this and that in his strange accent. Asdelar, for his part, seemed pleased to have a traveling companion willing to hold a lengthy conversation, and the two went on and on about nonsensical things as Hinego tried his best to ignore them and keep one eye on the sky for Dora. It was a bit heartening that he at last had something to add to his report, even if none of it was substantial evidence.

Asdelar was laughing at something the Rover had said, and Fikin was laughing with him as if they were old friends. Hinego scowled darkly at their backs. One cheerful talkative traveling companion was hard enough, but at least he'd developed some sort of trust for Asdelar. He was still irked at the Rover's presence, but since he had already agreed to let him travel with them, there was nothing he could do about it now without looking the fool. He kept his mouth shut and tried to tune out their banter, determined to be mature and serene about the whole thing.

So of course that was when it started raining.

It began as a light drizzle, the cool drops almost pleasant, and quickly turned into a deluge. It dampened even Asdelar's spirits, and they trudged on grimly, barely able to see more than a few yards in any direction. It was a spring storm: sudden and quick. It was gone within an hour, but by then the three men were soaked to the bone and shivering. Fikin tried to make light conversation again, but

Asdelar was too wet and miserable to humor him, which gave Hinego a mean-spirited satisfaction.

It was just over a four hour ride to the nearest village, and with clouds still lingering, the sun did little to either warm or dry them. It was a sorry looking trio that rode into the small village of Pran. Asdelar immediately began looking about for an inn, obviously hoping for a chance to get a hot meal in his stomach and dry clothes on his back. Hinego shared the desire for simple comforts, but he was made of sterner stuff.

"We'll just ask around for information and then be on our way," he declared, pulling his mare up alongside Asdelar's stallion as they picked their way down the muddy road. "We wasted enough time at the Crossroads, and the storm slowed us down a bit as well."

"Oh have a heart, Imalt-wor," Fikin wheedled—more for Asdelar's sake than his own, Hinego was certain. "It'll be evening in a few hours. Why not stop here for a bit?"

Hinego offered him a cool look. "I would think a Rover would be used to the discomforts of the outdoors," he pointed out. "We can sleep on the side of the road tonight."

"That's a good way to get robbed, that is," Fikin advised.

"We will sleep in shifts," Hinego said curtly. "Not that I think many bandits would take their chances with a group that obviously has an Imalt-wor with them."

Asdelar arched a brow at him, but didn't mention the ambush in the alley back in Amsdale. "Hinego's right," he sighed, surprising Hinego a bit. "We need to keep moving." He reached back past Fikin's thigh and patted the saddlebags, tilting his chin towards the small open market further down the road. "Though we do need to resupply. What if I stop by the vendors while you go ask pointed, uncomfortable questions? You're better at it anyhow." He smiled, but it was a bit lopsided. Despite his words, he was obviously deeply regretting the loss of a warm bed.

Hinego didn't feel at all guilty. Their duty to the crown came first.

He told himself this three times as he slid from his mare and set off in the other direction to seek out any hints of Lady Valera's passing.

He gave her description to everyone he passed, asking the same questions he had of Rinara's caravan. When he had no luck on the streets, he tried the village's sole inn, a squat ugly building that was just as unimpressive on the inside as it was on the outside.

And here the gods finally had a bit of pity on him.

"We gets all manner of men passin' through here," the innkeeper admitted dubiously, scratching at the stubble on his chin and squinting at the ceiling in a speculative way as Hinego stood waiting patiently. "Can't tell you how many shifty-lookin' folks I've seen in my day ... Wait, I think I do remember a girl. Small little thing, red hair, y'said?"

"Yes." Hinego put his hands atop the bar eagerly, despite his earlier promise to himself not to touch any of the obviously unwashed surfaces in the inn's smoky tavern. "You saw her? When?"

"Aye, I saw a little snip of a girl, about two weeks back, I think. Maybe less. Looked a bit snooty to me. She didn't say much. No, the ones she was with, they was the ones who did all the talkin'."

"How many were with her?"

"Hmm, can't say for sure ..." the man trailed off thoughtfully.

Hinego slapped a coin on the counter, but kept his finger over it firmly, waiting.

"Five men. Real sly-lookin' fellas, too. They kept to their room, mostly, them and the girl."

"Did they stay long?"

"Just a night. They looked to be in some sort of hurry to me. I think they said they were headin' south. That's all I know."

Hinego relinquished the coin and left to find his companions.

~~*

"Your friend's a bit prickly, ent he?" Fikin noted as he pawed absently through the fruit on display at one vendor's stall. "Not that I've met many friendly Reds before."

Asdelar reached out and plucked away the apple that had been about to disappear into one of the many folds in Fikin's clothes.

Fikin laughed sheepishly. "Sorry, force of habit," he said in an undertone, checking to make sure the vendor hadn't noticed.

Asdelar checked the apple for bruises, then tucked it into his bag with the others and paid for the lot. "Hinego takes a bit of getting used to," he admitted with a grin. "Most Imalt-wor I've met have seemed a bit stand-offish, but not all of them. I think it's just part of his personality to be so ..."

"Unbearable?" Fikin offered cheekily.

"Stiff," Asdelar finished. "He's not that bad once

you get to know him. Or maybe I've just gotten accustomed to it. He is *so* easy to bait, after all, which can be quite entertaining at times."

Fikin laughed at that. "So what about you, Asdelar Lorem?" he asked, reaching out to tuck a lock of wayward blond hair behind Asdelar's ear. "Why are you in the company of a Red on a quest? You're obviously not Imalt-wor, but I've never known 'em to travel in the company of noblemen." Again his eyes flickered to the sword on Asdelar's belt as they moved on to the next vendor. "They'll defend them, aye, even go with 'em for a bit on the roads for protection. But somehow I don't see you as the kind to hire a bodyguard. And he doesn't strike me as the bodyguard type, either. There's more goin' on here than you're lettin' on. Whatever his mission is, you seem to be in on it."

"Maybe I just enjoy his company," Asdelar teased, paying for two loaves of coarse bread.

Fikin grinned, not fooled for a minute. "Be that as it may, you're holdin' back on me, Asdelar. We're goin' to be together for a few days yet. Don't you think I should know what I might be gettin' meself into by travelin' with you?"

"I'm sorry, Fikin," Asdelar said reluctantly.

Fikin sighed dramatically, but seemed to accept that he would be getting no answers for the time being. "All right, be secrety, then. I'll just console myself with the fact that we'll be sharin' a blanket under the stars tonight."

"Oh will we?" Asdelar murmured, amused.

Fikin smiled winningly. "Oh, aye, it will be very romantic. Might as well make the best of our little camp out, don't you think?"

Asdelar shook a finger in the grinning man's face. "You, sir, are a bit too charming for your own good."

Fikin captured the finger in his hand, refusing to relinquish his grip when Asdelar pulled back reflexively. "All us Rover types are, didn't you know that?" He shifted closer, lowering his voice and smiling in a conspiratorial way. "I know I'm your type, Asdelar. And you're certainly mine."

"You're certainly very sure of yourself," Asdelar retorted, but couldn't help but smile back. "How do you know what my type is?"

"I'm everybody's type."

Asdelar laughed, but stopped trying to tug his finger free.

"Am I interrupting something?"

Asdelar jumped, spinning around with an unnecessary flush of guilt.

Hinego was watching the both of them from just a few feet away, eyes hooded, expression barely tolerant. "Are you finished shopping, or did you two need a few minutes alone?" he asked with a slight edge to his voice. "Because I've actually got us some useful information for a change."

Fikin released Asdelar's finger and offered Hinego an insulting smile. "Well you've already ruined the moment, ent you? Might as well tell us what's so important."

Hinego gave him a long look just this side of threatening. "You'd do well to respect your betters, Rover."

"You point 'em out to me, Red, an' I'll be sure to."

Hinego bristled.

"Could we not start a fight right in the middle of the street, gentlemen?" Asdelar demanded, stepping hastily in between them. "What did you find out, Hinego?"

Hinego forced his gaze from Fikin and turned away, leading his mare. "The innkeeper saw the girl just two weeks ago, in the company of some unsavory-looking men. They've got a big head start on us. We have to go."

"I don't take well to uppity men," Fikin remarked under his breath as he helped Asdelar quickly load the saddlebags.

"Leave him be," Asdelar insisted. "Anyway, he's right. We need to get moving. Come on."

~~*

They were all still damp and uncomfortable, but the news of Lady Valera's sighting heartened both Gravemen. Even Fikin was affected by their quiet urgency and kept the light-hearted conversation and teasing to a minimum for the rest of the afternoon.

Hinego pressed them as hard as Asdelar's overburdened horse would allow and did not call a halt until the moon had risen. Secretly Asdelar was certain that they might have been bullied onwards throughout the night if not for the risk of a horse stumbling in the dark.

Hinego had chosen their campground well, however. Despite his own confidence in keeping bandits at bay with the sight of his sash alone, he was not brazen enough to camp right there beside the open road. The grasslands, seemingly flat as a plane of glass at first glance, hid many pockets and sudden hills, most of them invisible beneath the wild grass until one was right upon them. Hinego had been riding just off the road keeping his sharp eyes peeled for just such a thing, and when he led them off the road a little ways and down a slope, the road disappeared from view. Asdelar nodded in approval as he dismounted. No one would see them from the road, and unless one was looking for the small bowl-shaped clearing, they would never find it.

Hinego immediately put Fikin to work building a small fire with what few twigs and dried brush could be found while he and Asdelar tended to the horses and spread the sleeping blankets out.

"I meant what I said before, Lorem," Hinego said quietly, glancing towards where Fikin was foraging for tinder. "You keep an eye on that fool. For all we know he has some of his friends following a few hours behind us who plan to ambush us in the night."

"You're being paranoid, Hinego," Asdelar chided, choosing a simple dinner from the groceries he had purchased in Pran. "I think he's a nice enough man. Give him a chance."

"I'll give him a boot to the head if he tries anything funny," Hinego swore.

"I'll watch him, all right? I like him—"

"I noticed."

"... But I'm not completely daft." Asdelar grinned at him. "And what does it matter to you anyhow whether or not I like the man? Why, Hinego, if I didn't know you any better, I'd think you were jea—"

"I just don't want you letting your personal feelings get in the way of common sense," Hinego snapped irritably.

Asdelar sidestepped, cutting the other man off when he moved towards the horses. "Come on, Hinego, quit being such a fussbudget." When Hinego reached past him stubbornly and began untying his canteen from his saddle, Asdelar slipped his hand between Hinego's arms, laying his palm comfortably on the inside his elbow. "You know I like you best," he teased with a grin.

Hinego pulled away, canteen in hand, and made a face at him. Before he could voice an undoubtedly blistering retort, Fikin came strolling up with an armload of pitiful twigs and dried grass.

"Cuddent find much," he admitted, smoothly walking between the two of them and forcing Asdelar to back away from Hinego. "Further down south there's less grasslands an' more trees. Here it's a good idea to carry your own fuel. This ent really enough for much more 'n a bit of light."

Hinego answered that by pulling two dark lumps out of one of his bags, each a bit bigger than a man's hand.

Asdelar got a faint whiff of the things and wrinkled his nose in distaste. "Is that what I think it is?"

"Horse manure's great in fire," Fikin said approvingly as he arranged the tinder and then took the cakes from Hinego and added them to the pile. "The fire might smell funny, but it'll burn a bit longer an' brighter."

"There's some oil and braided cord in there, as well as some other things," Hinego explained to Asdelar, who was still making a face. "The Imalt-wor uses them when firewood is scarce, like here on the grasslands. It will smell, yes, and I wouldn't advise cooking anything with it. But it will get rid of the chill. Speaking of which, we'd best change into something dry and let these clothes air out overnight."

Asdelar sighed, plucking at the front of his damp shirt. "Why is it that I am in constant need of changing into dry clothes on this trip?"

Fikin, who had brought only a small sack of belongings, had only one spare outfit, and refused to change into it. "I'll need it in Nehalm," he protested. "I'll be snug enough in one of these blankets."

Hinego shrugged, as if unconcerned with whether or not Fikin chose to risk getting sick. He and Asdelar changed, and Fikin stripped down completely and wrapped himself up in one of the blankets. The fire was started and a cold meal of jerky, bread, and cheese was passed around, with apples for dessert.

Asdelar shifted, trying to get upwind of the pungent fire, and glanced at each of his companions. Neither was speaking, eating their simple meal in grim silence while shooting each other the occasional distrusting look. Asdelar sighed internally and attempted to take on the role of peacemaker.

"So, Fikin, why are you headed for Nehalm? Do you have family there?"

"The caravan is my family," Fikin pointed out with a small smile. "No, I have business there, nothin' more."

"Houses to rob, people to scam?" Hinego muttered, not quite quietly enough.

Fikin ignored him. "I might expand on the subject if you'd be willin' to tell me what this 'orribly important mission of yours is."

Asdelar hastily changed the subject. "Er, so you've done a fair amount of traveling as a Rover, correct? What's it like out west? I've never been."

Fikin stretched languidly, tossing his apple core into the fire. "Not much to tell. Mostly farmland.

Everywhere you go things're a bit diff'rent. Dress, customs, land. It's definitely hotter out west. Makes travelin' a bit harsh sometimes." He smiled sideways at Asdelar. "Y'know, there *are* better ways to get to know a person more intimately."

Asdelar missed the hint completely—for once—because the Rover's words had just given him an idea. "Of course! Truth or Fancy!"

Fikin pouted a bit, then cocked his head curiously. "What's that, now? What're you so excited about?"

"Truth or Fancy," Asdelar repeated, eager to get the two men to participate. "It's a game. I've played it once or twice. Actually, isn't it—"

Hinego nodded, frowning in displeasure. "The Imalt-wor invented it, probably on some bored rainy night when a few squads were stuck indoors together. It's a way to get to know each other."

"A form of Faew-bor?" Asdelar guessed with a grin.

"Sort of. The game is useful, but a bit childish. I hope you don't expect us to play."

"Why not? It will be fun, and we'll learn some interesting things about each other!"

"Assuming we're all being truthful," Hinego drawled. "Which is unlikely. Besides, it's a drinking game, and we don't have any—"

"Ah." Fikin reached into his sack and triumphantly presented an earthenware jar. "Did ye forget who you're with? Rovers always got a bit of rum or wine on them, even if it means leavin' behind the water."

"No," Hinego said flatly at Asdelar's hopeful look.

"Oh, come on, it won't be like last time," Asdelar wheedled. "You don't have to drink as much. Besides, you're only supposed to take a drink—"

"Every time you guess incorrectly. I know how the game is played. No, Lorem."

"Well I don't know how it's played," Fikin butted in.

"It's simple," Asdelar explained, throwing a wounded look Hinego's way. "We each take turns. Let's say I'm first. I would tell you both something about myself, either a truth or a lie. Then you two guess whether I'm being honest or not. It shows how well you know a person, or it helps you get to know a person better. If you guess wrong, you take a drink. If you both guess correctly, I take a drink for being outwitted."

"Sounds like fun to me," Fikin agreed readily, uncorking the rum. He glanced at Hinego out of the corner of his eye. "Leave this one out of it," he purred. "'E seems a bit afraid to talk about hisself. You and I can drink and ... get to know each other."

"Are you calling me a coward?" Hinego demanded.

"You said it, not I," Fikin said lightly, and bared his teeth in a fierce smile. "If I'm wrong, prove it, Red." He thrust the jar towards Hinego. "You go first."

Hinego glared first at the jar, then at Fikin, back rigid.

"He doesn't have to play if he doesn't want to," Asdelar relented, reaching for the jar. "Hinego doesn't like drinking, anyhow."

"Oh, I see," Fikin said innocently, but his eyes were mocking.

Hinego's lip curled, and abruptly he reached out and snatched the jar away. "Only a couple of rounds," he snapped.

"If you say so."

Asdelar smiled, pleased at his reluctant cooperation. "Go ahead, Hinego: truth or fancy?"

Hinego hesitated, glaring at the jar as he mulled it over. He thought for so long that Asdelar was beginning to think he'd changed his mind, when he finally said shortly, "I am third generation Imalt-wor."

"True," Fikin said after a moment's deliberation.

Asdelar grinned, wondering if Hinego had purposefully chosen a topic he'd just discussed with Asdelar, or if he was simply at a loss for subject matter. "False."

Hinego handed the jar wordlessly to Fikin.

"Oh ho, I am a bit surprised," Fikin admitted, taking a quick swig of the spicy rum. "I assumed you were following in your old man's footsteps, an' his father afore him, an' so on. All right then, it's my turn. Let's see ..." He tapped a finger against his jaw, musing under his breath. "Ah, here we go. I am father of an illegitimate child."

"True," Hinego said without hesitation, his lip curling.

Asdelar arched a brow. "False."

"Y'got a knack for this game," Fikin chuckled, then held the jar out to Hinego again. "Y'really think so little of me an' my kind, Red?"

Hinego declined to comment, taking an unwilling sip and passing it to Asdelar.

"I've got one ready," Asdelar declared, grinning from ear to ear. "I'm curious to see what each of you thinks." He held the jar up and glanced from one man to the other. "I don't have a single scar on my body."

"True," Fikin said easily, obviously going off of the assumption that Asdelar was a pampered nobleman, but eyeing him in a way that suggested he would like to find out the truth of the matter for himself.

Hinego hesitated, considering what skill Asdelar had claimed to have with the blade. "False," he said at last.

"Where is this scar?" Fikin demanded as the jar was pressed into his hands. "I don't suppose you'd show us some proof?"

Asdelar laughed and held out his hands to display the many small bumpy scars: proof of clumsiness with a sharp blade, most of them undoubtedly from training.

"Well of course the Red would get that one right, then," Fikin grumbled.

"Why would I look that closely at his hands?" Hinego snapped, and found the jar hovering in front of his face once again.

"Your turn, Red. An' try to think of a more interestin' question than your last one, eh?"

Hinego took the rum, prepared this time. "I've never killed anyone," he said, looking directly at Fikin.

The cheerfulness in Fikin's tight smile faded somewhat, turning into something colder. "False."

"False," Asdelar agreed quietly.

Hinego took his drink. "I have," he admitted, flicking Asdelar a sharp look. "But you haven't."

"How could you possibly—"

"It hangs over a man's head like a cloud for anyone to see if they're looking for it," Hinego said, staring at the jar. "You've never killed a man." He shrugged, relinquishing the jar to Fikin. "Besides, you balked at the thought of killing those thieves who accosted you at the inn a few days back. That was a big hint."

Asdelar frowned, but Fikin was already speaking.

"Nothin' wrong with not havin' taken a life, Asdelar," he said firmly, tousling Asdelar's hair. "Makes you a bigger man than either of us, I say."

Asdelar stared at him, then shot a quick look at Hinego, who didn't look at all surprised at the Rover's veiled admittance to murder.

Perhaps sensing Asdelar's discomfort, Fikin started the next round on a lighter note. The jar passed hands, rum was swallowed in increasing amounts, and Asdelar was able to glean a few interesting facts about his companions.

Like the fact that Fikin was ambidextrous, could peel an apple in one long unbroken strip, and had never in his life tasted the expensive white bread sold in the cities, though he planned to remedy that at some point.

Hinego had learned to ride a horse when he was twelve, demonstrated that he could balance Fikin's reluctantly loaned dagger on his fingertip for a full minute, and was the fourth of five children, though he was the only one who had joined the Imalt-wor.

The fire was dying and the moon was high in the night sky when Hinego announced it was time to stop the foolishness and get some shut-eye. He frowned in disapproval as a giggling Asdelar nearly toppled onto his side. "Do you never learn?" he demanded. "You're going to get sick."

"As I recall," Asdelar said loftily, "it was you who couldn't handle your spirits last time."

Hinego glared and said nothing.

"I think someone's been skimping," Fikin accused. "You 'aven't been drinkin' as much on your turns, Red." He paused to belch, then sat very still for a few moments to make sure the contents of his stomach didn't decide to come up as well.

"Unlike you imbeciles, I have no wish to drink myself into a stupor," Hinego said with a sniff. "Get up, Lorem, you look daft. Give me the rum."

Asdelar managed to hold it out of reach, grinning widely at the other man. "One more round, Hinego," he insisted. "And pick a good one this time. Something neither of us could possibly know."

"I'm not—"

Asdelar held the jar close to his mouth as if about to drain the rest.

"Fine," Hinego growled, snatching it away. "This is the last one. I mean it."

"Then y'have t'finish th' rum," Fikin slurred. "If there's enny left ... We still go."

Hinego glared at him.

"Make it a good one," Asdelar said again, prodding him playfully.

"What do you mean a 'good' one? Stop poking me, idiot."

"Something I won't be able to guess." Asdelar grinned. "Something you know I want to know. Like ... I don't know." He waved his hands in the air, grasping at straws. "You're ... secretly a woman."

Fikin burst into braying laughter and fell onto his back where he continued to snicker.

Hinego glanced at the jar in his hand, hesitating.

"Come onnn, Hinego," Asdelar whined. "Just one little thing, anything. But if it's not good—"

Hinego's voice was low and terse, unheard by the chortling Rover in the grass. "I've never taken a man to my bed."

Asdelar shut his mouth on the rest of his interrupted protest so quickly that his teeth clicked.

He stared at Hinego, startled. Briefly, dark eyes flashed his way, though Hinego's expression was impossible to read.

Neither man was sure what prompted him to say those words. Perhaps it was the rum talking. Perhaps he was just positive that it was a riddle Asdelar could not possibly guess correctly.

But there was always, Asdelar thought with a sudden twist of hope, the small chance that it was ... something else.

A hint, perhaps?

Or just the opposite, he told himself with an inner wince. If Hinego spoke the truth, it could be his way of hammering home the 'Stop flirting with me, idiot' message he'd been trying to bludgeon into Asdelar's head since day one.

Asdelar wrestled back and forth, unsure which guess was correct, then decided it didn't matter. He would have his answer, no matter what his guess was.

"False," he said, watching Hinego closely.

Then suddenly Fikin was scrambling to get away from the fire, practically crawling over Asdelar's lap in the process. "OgodsI'mabouttobesicknowMOVE."

"Hey, easy there—!" Asdelar grappled with the man, trying to keep him from falling into the fire and get him off his lap at the same time.

Hinego rolled his eyes, tossing the jar towards Fikin's sack. "Finally, an end to this ridiculous game," he grumbled, getting to his feet and dusting himself off. "I'm going to get some sleep. If he's going to be sick, get him away from the camp."

"But—you—I mean—" Asdelar looked helplessly from him to the rum, but Hinego had already turned his back and was arranging his blanket to his liking.

Frustrated, but unable to ignore Fikin's pitiful mumbles and groans any longer, Asdelar pushed himself unsteadily to his feet and led him further away from the camp. He held Fikin's shoulders in support as he was violently sick in the grass, then helped him back to the fire. He wanted to question Hinego about the last round in the game, but he was already rolled up in his blanket with his back to them.

Sighing in defeat, Asdelar checked to make sure the fire was contained in its circle of dirt and made himself comfortable on his own blanket.

Well, he consoled himself, he could always ask about it later. Some sleep would do him good. It had been a long day, and if he hoped to forestall a hangover, he would have to grab as much shut-eye as he could.

"You've got first watch," Hinego reminded him sleepily without turning around. "That damned Rover had better still be here in the morning, Lorem, or I'm holding you responsible."

"But—"

"I don't snore," Fikin declared, barely coherent, a part of his muddied brain assuming they were still playing the game.

As it turned out, it was a bald-faced lie.

Chapter Ten

If Asdelar had held any hopes the game would help ease the tension between his companions, those hopes were quickly shot down by sunrise the next day and continued to plummet for the remainder of the day.

He had spent the majority of the journey teasing and baiting Hinego, but to see Fikin do it only made him sympathetic. Fikin seemed to find his new game immensely entertaining and heckled Hinego throughout the morning. Hinego managed to keep a leash on his temper for the most part, but every now and then he would snarl back a fierce retort. Asdelar guiltily promised himself he would not tease him so much in the future, then promptly forgot the vow an hour later.

"Why so grumpy, Red?" Fikin sneered, obviously delighted at having earned another outburst after his merciless badgering. "Didn't get enough sleep?"

"I wonder whose fault that is."

"You do snore," Asdelar said with a wry grin. "Rather loudly, in fact."

"I never!" Fikin feigned shock. "I sleep silent as the dead, I do."

"If you say so."

Hinego snorted loudly in derision.

Fikin retaliated by wrapping his arms more firmly

around Asdelar's waist from where he rode behind him. He returned Hinego's dark look with a cheeky smile.

"You won't fall off," Asdelar assured him over his shoulder, misreading the move. "Have you never ridden a horse before?"

Fikin shrugged, refusing to slacken his comfortable grip. "Once or twice. Horses are too expensive, and they're not as tough as mules. Big beasts. I feel too far off the ground."

"You're not a bad rider," Asdelar complimented. "I've seen worse."

Hinego cut in before Fikin could twist that innocent statement around. "There's a rest stop just ahead. We'll stop for a moment to water the horses and make sure we're still on the right track."

"A rest stop?" Asdelar looked at him in confusion, already reaching for his map. "How do you know?"

Hinego pointed at a slender stick thrust in the dirt alongside the road, a red ribbon flapping from its end. "That's a makeshift sign post. A band of Imalt-wor is doing a customs check on this road. It's customary to do so every hundred miles or so, to weed out smugglers and look for bounties. This group must have come from Lehaim." He stopped suddenly, suspicion and surprise flashing across his face before he carefully concealed his emotions. "Later," he mouthed when Asdelar sent him a curious look.

As Hinego had predicted, two miles down the road they came across a pair of tents and a small band of Imalt-wor. Two were on horseback off the side of the road, obviously ready to pursue anyone stupid enough to attempt to rush through. They nodded in recognition of a fellow Red as Hinego led the way towards the man waiting just outside one of the tents.

Fikin looked increasingly uneasy as they approached, and Hinego seized the opportunity to get him out of his hair. "Water the horses," he ordered, nodding towards a trough as he dismounted. "We'll take care of this."

Looking relieved, Fikin jumped down and led the horses towards the water as Hinego and Asdelar approached the customs officer.

"You're not required to stop," the big man said, eyes on Hinego's red sash. "Feel free to move on once you've rested your horses."

"We need information," Hinego said, looking to make sure Fikin was out of earshot. "Lord Stimad's daughter is missing, and we have reason to suspect foul play. There's a possibility she might have gone south. You came from Lehaim, didn't you?"

"Jorwa, actually," the officer said, scratching absently at his chest. "We were stationed there until last month. Business as usual down there. Cutthroats, thieves, and murderers." He scowled. "Longest three months of my life." He looked skyward, searching his memory. "Don't recall stumbling across any hint of ransom for anyone high-born. We might have passed her on the road, though. She's blond, isn't she? I've never seen her myself."

"Redhead," Asdelar corrected. "A little on the small side."

"We made monthly trips up to Lehaim for supplies and reports. Is that where you think she might be headed?"

"It's a possibility," Hinego affirmed.

"Best speak to Turshy, then." The big man nodded

towards one of the Reds on horseback. "She was the liaison between the crown and Count Gray."

"Thank you." Hinego steered Asdelar away.

"Count Gray?" Asdelar repeated blankly.

"I can't believe I didn't think of Lehaim before," Hinego muttered to himself. "If she's under duress and still headed south, that's the most likely place she's headed."

"Wait." Asdelar grabbed his elbow to pull him to a stop. "Hinego, you aren't making any sense. Who's Count Gray? What's in Lehaim? I'm not sure I've ever heard of it."

"It's a small territory," Hinego explained, keeping his voice low. "Ervin Gray served in the war with the King's father and displayed great loyalty and valor. He was rewarded with a title, and given some land in the south: Lehaim. It hasn't done so well lately because Jorwa, a smaller town in the territory, has become a haven for criminals in the past fifteen years. Ervin's mental health is said to have been deteriorating for years, and his son, Rewen Gray, is the current Count. It's no secret Rewen holds some kind of grudge against the King for giving his family what he considers useless land. He's never said so publicly, of course, but the Imalt-wor always keep a close eye on him when they're stationed anywhere nearby."

"I don't see what this has to do with the Lady Valera," Asdelar protested.

Hinego frowned at him. "Use your head. What if that idiot Count has decided to make a move against the King by kidnapping her? Everyone knows His Majesty dotes on her."

"That would be insane!" Asdelar exclaimed. "The King would crush him!"

"Right now everyone assumes the Lady Valera simply ran away," Hinego pointed out. "If she disappears forever without a trace, the King will be heartbroken, but there will be no proof of Count Gray's involvement."

"You're making a lot of dangerous accusations and assumptions," Asdelar said slowly. "What if the Count has nothing to do with her disappearance?"

"That's what we need to find out," Hinego said firmly. "If that's where she's headed, we need to make sure Gray pays for it. On the slim possibility that she really is simply rebelling against her family, she might stop by Lehaim if she's heard of the Count's grudge. Either way, Lehaim is our best bet. If not there, then Jorwa. They're exactly the type of scum to ransom a girl, or even sell her."

"All right," Asdelar agreed, "you've made your point. But you shouldn't start throwing these accusations about once we reach Lehaim. If you're wrong and we offend the Count, we're in for it."

"I can be discreet," he said huffily.

Asdelar tried and failed to hide a smile. "Still, I think it best if I do the talking in Lehaim."

He began to argue, but Asdelar was already striding past him.

"Excuse me, madam," he said with all his charm as he smiled up at the grim-faced Red on horseback. "Would you be Miss Turshy?"

"That's me," the woman said briskly, visibly unimpressed by the bright smile. "Who's asking?"

"Asdelar Lorem of the Banam-hin." He executed a brief but fancy bow. "I understand you were the crown's liaison for Lehaim?"

Turshy looked from him to Hinego before

answering. "That's right."

Asdelar briefly explained their mission and described Lady Valera. Turshy leaned her elbow against her saddle horn and gazed at him steadily for a few moments as she digested the news. "I never saw her," she said at last. "I did overhear something strange once in the Count's mansion, however. The butler was giving orders to the servants about setting up a room. Something about a female guest the Count was expecting. As soon as they saw me in hearing range, they stopped talking."

"Interesting," Hinego mused. "And you never passed a girl on the road?"

The other horseman shook his head. "Not fitting that description. There's always the possibility she stayed off the road to prevent being seen. She would have had to go almost a mile out of her way to do so, though. It will give you an edge if she's not that far ahead of you."

Hinego thanked them and called for Fikin to bring the horses. Turshy and her partner watched Fikin keenly, but made no move to stop him as he climbed up behind Asdelar and they continued down the road.

Fikin let out a sigh of relief once the small Imalt-wor camp was far enough behind them.

"Why so nervous, Fikin?" Hinego demanded, glaring at him. "Should I have let them search you?"

"Search me yourself," Fikin challenged, lifting his chin in defiance. "I ain't carryin' anything illegal. The law just makes me uneasy, is all."

"Fikin, be honest with us," Asdelar said quietly. "Is there anything we should know?"

"Don't be silly," Fikin laughed. "It's just bred into

us Rovers not to trust the crown, I swear. I'll be out of your hair for good when we reach Nehalm."

"There's been a change of plans," Hinego said curtly. "We won't be passing through Nehalm. We have business further south. We'll part ways in Belor."

Fikin looked disappointed, and Hinego was unsure whether the expression was genuine or not. "That's not much time left together," Fikin complained. He wrapped his arms around Asdelar's waist once more, lowering his voice. "I suppose I'll have to make the best of the time we've got left, eh?"

Asdelar didn't answer, but Hinego noticed his ears had gone quite red.

Oddly irritated, Hinego rode ahead so he would not have to look.

~~*

The next five days felt like the longest of Hinego's life. He had not realized how accustomed he had become to Asdelar's rambling conversations until they were gone.

It wasn't that Asdelar didn't talk—it was just that Fikin went out of his way to take up the lion's share of his attention. The two laughed and talked together endlessly, with Hinego riding further and further ahead to tune them out until he was left out of conversations entirely. Hinego's mood grew increasingly sour until Asdelar gave up any attempts to speak to him when they camped at night. By the third night Hinego had completely isolated himself socially from the two.

He told himself angrily he should be grateful neither of them were talking his ear off. But Fikin's blatant interest and his successful attempts to keep Asdelar to himself got under Hinego's skin. He would be glad to be rid of him.

And it wasn't as if Asdelar was exactly letting Fikin down. Asdelar was his normal friendly, borderline flirtatious self around him.

Good, Hinego thought fiercely. *It keeps the idiot from messing with my head.*

Still, his mood was dark when they finally rode into Belor on the evening of the fifth day.

Asdelar had been oddly quiet all afternoon, sending questioning looks his way. As soon as they handed their horses over to the stable boy at the local inn, he turned to Fikin and said firmly, "Why don't you go get our rooms and order us some supper? I need to speak with Hinego."

Fikin sent Hinego a sideways look, but took the coins Asdelar handed over and went into the inn without protest.

Being alone with Asdelar was the last thing Hinego wanted. "I'm going to ask around for information," he proclaimed, but Asdelar didn't let him get more than a few steps down the street before he dodged in front of him.

"Hinego, wait." Asdelar's expression was an odd twist of frustration and confusion. "Why have you been so antisocial lately? More than usual, I mean. Have I done or said something to offend you again? We can't work together if you're going to be so off-putting."

"There's nothing wrong," Hinego snapped, forcing himself to look Asdelar in the eye. "This trip is tiring and I'll be glad to have it finished, that's all. We should be in Lehaim soon, and then hopefully this whole thing will be over with. Move aside. I have inquiries to make."

"This has something to do with Fikin, doesn't it?" Asdelar demanded. "You haven't trusted or liked him since you first set eyes on him. We won't see him again after tonight when we go our separate ways. Can't you be civil for just one night? He hasn't done anything to deserve such animosity." His brows lowered. "And neither have I."

"I never said you did."

"But you've been avoiding me for days," Asdelar pointed out with an edge of anger to his normally cheery tone. "You've been cold towards both of us. You don't like that he and I are friends."

"Friends," Hinego scoffed.

"We *are*." Asdelar stopped suddenly, his eyes widening. "Wait. You don't like how he flirts with me, do you?"

Hinego pushed past him roughly. "Why would I care about that?"

"You tell me," Asdelar said quickly, grabbing his wrist to stop him.

He wrenched his hand away. "We're on a royal mission and you've got your head in the clouds," he growled. "Can't you keep it in your pants long enough to finish one simple quest? You're too distracted by that idiot Rover to keep your eye on our goal."

"Not this again!" Asdelar cried, looking hurt. "You still think that's all I think about? I never said I was interested in Fikin. I'm not blind—I know when I'm being flirted with. But I've told him not to expect anything. Not that it's any of your damned business anyway."

"No, it's not," Hinego said from behind clenched

teeth. "But since you brought it up, I do think that's what's always on your mind. You say it's not, but you flirt as easily as others draw breath. It's infuriating, and you're embarrassing yourself as much as me. Act with the dignity your position demands."

"I am not Imalt-wor!" Asdelar shouted in his face. "My personality was not beaten out of me in training, and my loyalty to the crown does not encompass every facet of who I am or what I do. I'm fully aware of my mission, and I am just as good at my job as you are at yours. How many tight spots do we need to get into for me to prove it to you?" He stopped and drew a steadying breath. "Tell me the truth," he said in a quieter voice. "Are you disgusted with me on principle, or are you just angry that Fikin and I flirt harmlessly with each other?"

Hinego's eyes dropped unwittingly, his voice low and harsh. "Everything about you is infuriating."

Asdelar took a step back and looked at him for a long moment, his mouth drawn in a tight, grave line. "I am through trying to puzzle you out," he said at last. "I am tired of trying to get past your defenses when all you do is lash out. I think things will be easier if I just take everything you say and do at face value, since that's obviously the only way you ever see me." He turned sharply on his heel and strode back to the inn.

Hinego watched him go in silence, fists clenched by his sides. He had a sudden wild impulse to stop Asdelar, but choked back the call bitterly. What would he say, anyway?

As he stood fuming in the street, he slowly became aware of the fact that he had an audience.

A shopkeeper was standing on her porch, leaning

on her broom and watching him with the intense interest of small town folk. "Lover's quarrel?" she asked sympathetically.

A rush of heat made Hinego's cheeks burn. "Mind your own business," he snarled, and stormed off.

"Young people these days," the woman tutted to herself, and continued sweeping her porch.

~~*

Hinego didn't show up for supper, so Asdelar icily suggested they eat and retire without him.

Fikin, though obviously curious about Asdelar's sudden bad mood, agreed without protest, and they spent the mealtime in awkward silence.

There was still no sign of Hinego when they were finished, and when Asdelar, in no hurry to see him again, declared that he was ready for bed, Fikin wordlessly led the way upstairs to their rooms.

"It was cheaper just to get two rooms," he explained as he opened a door and indicated that Asdelar enter. "That stuck-up Red can have 'is own room. We'll share this one. It will give us a chance to talk, seein' as you were so oddly not-chatty during supper."

Asdelar muttered assent and went straight to the bed, throwing himself face down atop it and tugging the pillow over his head.

Fikin latched the door behind himself and observed Asdelar with a knowing grin. "I take it you and Sir Prissy had a fight?"

"Mmph," came the muffled reply.

Fikin came over and perched on the edge of the bed, rubbing a hand consolingly on Asdelar's back.

"Don't let him get you so upset now, As'. Come on, show us a smile."

Asdelar rolled over, pushing the pillow aside and gazing up at him. "Look, Fikin," he said a bit hesitantly, "I don't feel much like talking. I said some things to Hinego I might regret in the morning, and I've still got to deal with him for the duration of our journey together. It's been a long day and I just want to sleep."

"But we part ways in the morning," Fikin reminded him, stretching out to lie beside him on the narrow bed, his hand resting comfortably on Asdelar's stomach. "You really want to spend the rest of the time we have together sulking?"

Asdelar forced a smile. "I'm sorry. I'm just not very good company right now."

Fikin propped his head up on his hand to look down at him curiously. "You like this Hinego fellow, don't you?"

Asdelar's eyes shied away. "That man's impossible to befriend. He has no tolerance for me."

"Let's not talk about him, then," Fikin declared. "It will only upset you more. In fact, let's not talk at all." He leaned over quickly and pressed his mouth to the side of Asdelar's throat.

"Uh—wait—" Asdelar grasped Fikin's shoulder and pushed him away, rolling onto his side so they were face-to-face. "Fikin, I told you I just want us to be friends."

"Yes, an' I guessed why," Fikin said dryly, his fingers wriggling under Asdelar's shirt. "But obviously that hardheaded Red doesn't care for you, in friendship or otherwise." He landed another brief kiss on Asdelar's jaw. "I, on the other hand, 'ave made my interests perfectly clear." He slid his hand further under the shirt so that his fingers were splayed against a tense abdomen. "And I was under the impression that you weren't too averse to the idea yourself."

Asdelar hesitated, and Fikin took the opportunity to steal a quick, sloppy kiss. "If the Red wants to act like a jealous child, let 'im," he murmured, trying to maneuver Asdelar onto his back. "Neither of you will see me again after tonight."

"Wait." Asdelar reached down quickly to seize the hand making its way south. "Jealous? He isn't jealous, he's just ... Why do you say jealous?"

Fikin frowned, obviously wishing he hadn't spoken. "Nothing. I meant nothing." He pressed up against him. "Never mind. He's obviously disgusted with you."

"Don't," Asdelar said firmly, pushing him away. "I mean it. Answer me, Fikin."

Fikin blew out an impatient sigh. "It just seems to me that he don't like the fact that I take up so much of your attention. He got used to havin' you to himself and then I showed up."

"He doesn't think that way," Asdelar protested weakly. "He's made it clear he can't stand how much I flirt, even when I don't mean to do it."

"Why would he like to see you flirtin' with anyone?" Fikin snorted, tugging at Asdelar's belt insistently. "Anyway, it was just a hunch. Obviously I was wrong, or else he's so deep in denial that I might as well be. Now, it's gettin' late. Will you stop talkin' and take off your clothes, or am I gonna have to tear them off?"

In a burst of frustration Asdelar shoved Fikin

harder than he meant to, sending him tumbling off the bed with a yelp.

"I said *no*," Asdelar snapped, sitting up quickly. "Am I going to have to trade rooms with Hinego, or are you going to keep your hands to yourself?"

Fikin stood up and put one knee on the bed, eyes narrowed. "Are you daft? The man's not interested! I can tell you're the type to take men to your bed, so what's your problem?" He spread his arms wide. "You've got someone willin' to share the night with you, and all you can think about is that insufferable donkey's ass!" He shrugged off his shirt and threw it aside. "Last chance, Asdelar. We'll prob'ly never see each other again. Are you really goin' to lie to yourself and say you don't want something to happen?"

"I do want something to happen," Asdelar admitted quietly, to himself as much as to Fikin. "But not with you."

Fikin snorted in disgust and walked over to where his shirt had fallen, snatching it up. "All right, fine. Be an idiot. Have fun tryin' to win over your precious Red."

"Where are you going?" Asdelar got up from the bed hastily. "I don't want to part on bad terms with you, Fikin. I'm still fond of you."

"I'll take the Red's room, an' after you two have spent the night fighting, maybe you'll see what a mistake you made," Fikin said harshly.

The door burst open suddenly, drowning out whatever protest Asdelar had been about to make.

There was a frozen moment of shocked silence as both men stared at the intruders. The four men in the doorway were concealing their faces with bandannas, and each of them carried a wickedly sharp knife.

The one in front glanced from Fikin to Asdelar and made a quick motion with his hand. "Kill the Imalt-wor," he grunted. "Take the Banam-hin alive."

Asdelar made a desperate leap for his sword, foolishly left on the table by the door, but he didn't make it in time.

~~*

Hinego was more than ready to get some food and sleep after almost two hours of asking after Lady Valera at just about every door in town. He'd made a circuit of the town and was nearly back where he'd started. He waited impatiently as the old man he was questioning hemmed and hawed thoughtfully after Hinego's brief line of questioning.

"No, haven't seen any girls like that," the old man finally declared. "Did see some right suspicious fellows hanging about the inn a little while ago, though. Looked pretty shady if you ask me."

Hinego felt a shiver of foreboding creep up his spine. "And you didn't think to tell anyone?" he demanded. "The town guard?"

"Was just minding my own business," the old man muttered, hobbling away. "Just told *you*, didn't I?"

Swearing an oath under his breath, Hinego made for the inn at a dead run.

He burst inside and immediately realized he was too late.

The innkeeper was speaking excitedly to a pair of town guardsmen while his wife stood white-faced behind the counter. The customers had all grouped together by the fire and were watching with interest.

"Hey, sir, you can't go up there!" one of the

guards shouted when Hinego dashed up the stairs. "There's been a crime here. Sir!"

"Shut it," his partner hissed hastily. "Are you blind? He's Imalt-wor."

Ignoring them, Hinego hurried down the upstairs hall until he came to a room being guarded by another officer of the law. "Move aside," he snarled. The guard put up a minimal protest, then fell back when the lantern light fell on the red sash across Hinego's chest.

Hinego barely noticed. He stood just inside the room, staring down in horror at the body crumpled on the floor beside the bed. The room was in total disarray. Someone had obviously put up quite a fight. A blanket had been thrown over the body, and it took longer than it should have for Hinego to force himself to walk across the room and drag the blanket aside to reveal the pale face underneath.

Fikin.

"Call a doctor!" he barked.

"One's been called, sir. He's on his way," the guard said hastily.

Hinego knelt beside Fikin and inspected him carefully. A stab to the chest area-- there was blood everywhere. He put his fingers quickly to Fikin's throat, feeling the faint pulse. Still alive, then. Lucky bastard. Whoever had stabbed him had aimed too high, missing the heart completely.

Wadding the blanket up, he pressed it firmly to the wound and looked around for any hint of who the attackers had been or what they'd been after. Where the hell was Asdelar, anyway? Had he gone looking for Hinego? He should have stayed here and looked after Fikin.

His eyes lit on the two pairs of boots carelessly thrown near the door, and he dragged unwilling eyes to the bare feet of the unconscious Rover.

Surely Asdelar wouldn't have run down the streets barefoot looking for him ..?

His heart was beginning to bang in his ears, and he faintly heard the guards in the hall conversing in hushed tones.

"The witnesses say they saw the men dragging a body out. Sounds like the blond who was staying here the night. No one was sure if he was alive or dead. Stable boy says they took his horse, too."

"Didn't anyone recognize them or see where they were going?"

"No, most of 'em said they hid. Didn't want any trouble."

"Figures."

"Make way, here comes the doctor!"

Hinego got numbly to his feet and turned to seize the doctor by his lapels as he came hurrying into the room.

"Wha—let go of me, fool," the doctor sputtered. "I've got to tend to your friend—"

"Save him," Hinego growled so fiercely the doctor went pale with fright. "Save his useless hide and let me know when he's conscious again. He might be the only proper witness we have to what happened here tonight."

~~*

The sun was high in the sky by the time Fikin was coherent enough to have visitors. The doctor hovered over him, checking his pulse and bandages as his nurses waited uneasily in the background and Hinego paced the floor behind him.

"My infirmary's not well-equipped for major surgeries such as this," the doctor said nervously, unable to meet the bloodshot stare of the Imalt-wor. "There's still the risk of infection or complications ..."

"So long as he can talk before he dies," Hinego cut him off heartlessly. He went to the bedside and glared down at its pathetic occupant. "Speak, Rover. And if you had anything to do with this, you'd better hope you die from infection."

Fikin blinked slowly up at him, still in a haze of pain. "You think I'd be lyin' in a hospital bed if I was in on it?" he asked in a raspy voice. "Go impregnate a horse, Red. I had nothing to do with that attack. Asdelar's my friend, too, you know."

"Then tell me what happened and who's responsible," Hinego commanded. "I searched the streets and the roads just outside town all night with no results. It's like they disappeared. So tell me everything you know."

Fikin closed his eyes wearily. "Don't know who they were," he muttered. "Four men ... masks ... Said to kill th' Red an' ... an' take the Blade. Guess they thought I was you. Stabbed me, left me there ... to die." He swallowed a few times, face flinching with pain. "They got Asdelar's sword, fought a bit ... Guess they won, 'cause I heard 'em talking. Said we were the ones who had been tailing 'em. Somethin' about ... a Count. A Count wantin' Asdelar for questioning. Don't know anything else."

Hinego's fists clenched convulsively, his jaw jerking in rage. "I knew it." He walked over to the window where a hawk was perched on the sill, making the nurses uncomfortable with its fierce stare. Writing quickly on a scrap of parchment, Hinego rolled up the message and attached it to the bird's leg when she climbed onto his arm. "Go, Dora," he said softly. "Fly swiftly." Throwing his arm out of the window, he released the hawk into the air, watching as she became nothing more than a speck in the sky.

He started towards the door, then seemed to change his mind and returned to the bed, where Fikin was starting to doze off again. Leaning over the wounded man, he lowered his voice to a threatening murmur. "And these men, did they take the time to strip you of your shirt?"

Fikin's eyes opened quickly, then shut again. He swallowed again, nervously this time. "Nothin' happened," he whispered. "Swear."

"No, I'm sure you were rudely interrupted." Hinego tensed as Fikin reached up feebly to grasp his sleeve, stopping him from leaving.

"Don't go yet." Fikin opened his eyes again to look Hinego in the face. "I want to go with you. Want to help Asdelar."

Hinego shook him off easily. "You're useless, and I don't have time to wait for you to heal anyway. Your part in this is over. If Asdelar wants to see you again, he'll visit when this is done with."

Ignoring the faint protests, he stepped outside into the tiny waiting room, where a town guardsman stood waiting for him uncertainly. "Sir, I just got a report in. A family of travelers entered the town just before dawn, and said they passed a group of horsemen heading south at full gallop. Said it looked like one was unconscious or wounded, draped over one of the horses. Might be your men."

"Good." Hinego rubbed roughly at his eyes. "There should be an Imalt-wor woman by the name of Morasa Ledyn looking for me in a few days. Tell her what's happened and that I've gone south to Lehaim. If she's brought her people with her, send them after me. Otherwise, have her wait here until I send word for her. If she stays in town for three days and has yet to receive a message from me, she's to alert the necessary authorities, then get her high and mighty behind down to Lehaim to pull mine out of the fire."

"Yes, sir. Er, are you sure you won't rest before you go? Maybe wait for reinforcements? You'll be put up for free room and board considering the circumsta—"

"No," Hinego cut him off. "The more I dawdle here, the further away they get. I'll sleep when this is done."

Without a backwards look, Hinego stalked outside, eyes snapping and back straight.

"Quite a character," the doctor observed from where he'd been eavesdropping in the doorway. "Are they all like that?"

"He's Imalt-wor," the guardsman said as if it were explanation enough. "Best just to get out of their way when they've got their blood up like that." He shuddered as if he'd felt a cool breeze. "If I were those men he's after, I'd be looking over my shoulder the whole way to Lehaim, waitin' for death to find me."

Chapter Eleven

Asdelar came to consciousness unwillingly, swamped by pain and confusion the instant his eyes cracked open.

For a fleeting moment he thought he'd had too much to drink and then fallen asleep riding again, slumped down against his horse's neck. A chafing on his wrists brought his attention to the rough ropes binding his hands to the saddle horn, and the memories of the previous night rushed back on the tail end of a splitting headache.

Fikin's rebuffed advances. The men bursting into the room. Fikin's blood everywhere ...

Trying to remain as still as possible and biting back a groan of pain, Asdelar craned his eyes to the left and right, straining to take in his surroundings from his near-prone position. He could just make out the rump of a horse a bit in front of him, the rider no doubt leading Asdelar's own mount by the reins. There was the sound of more riders behind him, just out of view. Staring down at the faint path in the grass, it took his addled brain longer than it should have to realize an alarming fact: they were no longer on the main road. This was practically a game path, faint and probably difficult to find. That meant if Hinego was tracking them, chances were they'd lost him the minute they left the King's Road. And Hinego *would* come after them. Wouldn't he? Asdelar shoved back the niggling self-doubts with a flare of impatient anger. Of course he would. He had to have figured by now that the kidnappers had something to do with Valera's disappearance. Following Asdelar would be his best chance of finding her.

Asdelar took a deep breath and forced himself to sit upright. One of the riders made a muffled sound of surprise, and he turned in his saddle to look back at them, hoping against hope that he would find Fikin similarly trussed up.

But the three men were unfamiliar to him, their faces hard and their clothing dark and inexpensive. The bandannas they'd worn during the attack were loose at their necks. Asdelar swallowed a few times, wishing fervently for water. "Where's my friend?" he demanded, his voice weaker than he liked.

One of the men gave a brutish laugh. "Dead as a doornail. You behave, or you'll get the same treatment."

The guilt and anger the news brought left Asdelar speechless for several heartbeats. "Why?" he finally managed to demand, teeth clenched. His head was beginning to pound. "What do you want?"

"This wouldn't have happened if the two of you hadn't insisted on tracking us," another man said.

"Jaks, enough," the leader snapped over his shoulder. He turned his pockmarked face towards Asdelar, scowling darkly. "The only reason you're alive is because our orders were to bring one of you in for questioning. Thank your lucky stars it was you and not your skinny friend. You give us too much trouble, though, and there might just be a violent accident on the road, you get me?"

Asdelar glared back mutely. He was briefly tempted to taunt them with the knowledge that they had failed, but he didn't want them looking back over their shoulders the whole way for an angry Imalt-wor. So he swallowed his guilt at the death of Fikin and said instead, "You're behind Lady Valera's disappearance, aren't you?"

"No more talking," the leader said, turning his back on Asdelar. "I'll gag you if I have to."

"That's my horse," Asdelar blurted indignantly, belatedly recognizing the stallion the leader rode as well as the packs of armor strapped behind the saddle.

The man glanced back briefly, yellowed teeth flashing in a smug smile. "Not anymore." He gave the horse a pat on the neck. "A fine beast." Laughing, he looked forward once more.

~~*

The men, though efficient fighters and kidnappers, were not professionals. Little respect was shown towards the leader, there was much complaining about the travel and brief breaks, and arguing broke out often, occasionally leading to the insulted parties getting down from their steeds to duke it out. It didn't take more than a few hours on the road to determine that they were nothing more notable than low-class mercenaries. The only things they seemed to be good at were brutality and keeping their mouths shut about their employer.

It was a day and a half of torment for Asdelar. His captors rarely remembered to give him water, let alone any scrap of food. They refused to unbind his hands, and the one time he attempted to make a break for it during the night, he was caught and beaten so badly he could barely sit upright in his saddle the next morning. When bored, the men taunted him about Fikin's death and offered many scalding opinions on the worthlessness of the King's Gravemen. Asdelar kept his mouth shut, refusing to rise to the bait.

He squinted at the landscape through swollen eyes, his tongue stuck to the roof of his mouth and his ribs screaming from the many kicks he'd received during his escape attempt. He swayed in his saddle, grim-faced and battered, beginning to feel nauseous from the lack of water and food. He was almost relieved when they approached what looked to be a small village, until the leader—aptly called Bruiser by his cohorts—leaned in to say, "Welcome to Jorwa, lordship."

Jorwa. The bandit's nest Hinego had mentioned. Ignoring his many pains, Asdelar forced himself to sit up in the saddle and look straight ahead. This was not a good place to show weakness.

It was a pitiful excuse of a town. Once it might have been like any other small town. There was a baker's shop and a forge, both of them long since abandoned. The roofs of many shops and houses had collapsed or rotted without proper care, very little glass remained in the windows, and the streets and alleys were filled with garbage and shifty-eyed inhabitants. The smell was atrocious, and the very air was thick with suspicious animosity. Scrawny whores lingered in doorways, watching the small party pass with sharp eyes and hard mouths. Sounds of fighting and cruel laughter came from the open tavern door, and all manner of weapons were very much in evidence.

Several men and women watched Asdelar like a hawk, fingering the daggers and cudgels in their belts, but Bruiser's reputation seemed to give them pause. Everywhere he looked, people quickly averted their eyes. One hopeful whore staggered drunkenly over, but one of Bruiser's men sent her sprawling in the dirt with a curse and a heavy kick to the chest that had the others barking with laughter. Asdelar clenched his fists and grit his teeth, but continued to stare straight ahead at nothing. With his hands tied and his sword in Bruiser's possession, there was little he could do should the people turn on him.

Hinego would have taken these guys out with both hands tied behind his back, he thought, and barely stopped the wistful smile that threatened to ease loose. Had Hinego picked up their trail? More importantly, had he thought to grab backup? Even he would have trouble in an entire village full of cutthroats. Surely he would at least bully some of Belor's town guard into accompanying him.

Not likely, he was forced to admit to himself. Hinego was stubborn and could be a bit impetuous. Asdelar could very easily imagine him marching boldly down Jorwa's dirty streets, coldly demanding cooperation from its black-hearted citizens. Idiot.

Slowly he became aware of the fact that his captors were arguing amongst themselves about what to do with him.

"I don't see why we can't have a few drinks first," Jaks was grumbling. "We deserve it after this job."

"We need a break," another wheedled. "We ain't slept in a real bed for days! We can tie this one up in a corner or somethin' until tomorrow."

"Shut your mouths," Bruiser snapped. He kicked the saddlebags with his heel, making the hidden armor clank. "First chance they get, some rat's going to make a go for our stuff. Might even take Sir High and Mighty here an' try ransoming him. We can rest after he's delivered and we're paid. One more complaint an' I'll take your cuts for myself!"

The threat earned him a few curses and nasty looks, but there were no more suggestions of a night's rest.

They stuck to the main road, clearly planning on passing right through. It wasn't long, however, before a small band of thieves decided to make a move, clearly unable to pass up the chance to make a few quick coins.

They came slinking out of a worn-down brothel, six sinister men with rusty knives and quick, darting eyes. They blocked the road and ordered Bruiser and his men to stop. One of them was slowly spinning a rope lasso by his side.

"Whatcher got there, Bruiser?" the biggest one called, eyeing the saddlebags greedily.

Bruiser slowed his horse to a slow walk, hand dropping to Asdelar's sword at his waist. "Out of the way, Roko. We're on official business. You know what'll happen if you interfere."

"Official business," Roko sneered, spitting in the dirt. "Don't make me laugh. You really think the Count cares if you lot end up dead in an alley? You're just hired muscle."

Asdelar took in a quick breath through his nose. The Count had hired these men. Did that mean Hinego had been correct in his theory? Was the man really so stupid he would risk the King's wrath by kidnapping Valera?

"He'll care this time," Bruiser insisted. "He's itchin' to ask this one some questions. He'll send someone lookin' for him if we don't show up."

"Maybe," Roko admitted, smiling like a serpent. "But not for you. I don't think he'll mind if *we* do the deliverin' instead." He motioned to his men, and they began to circle around the horses.

Bruiser didn't hesitate. He slammed his heels into his horse's flanks, yanking Asdelar's sword free of its scabbard simultaneously. The stallion leapt forward, and Roko barely managed to dive out of the way. The man with the lasso reacted quickly, flinging his rope out and slipping it neatly over Asdelar's horse as it was pulled along after Bruiser. The sudden jolt yanked the reins out of Bruiser's hands, and the horse shied, alarmed and confused.

With a yell, Asdelar slipped from the saddle. The ropes around his wrists held firm to the saddle horn, and he yelled again in pain as they tightened brutally. Feet dragging on the ground, he struggled to take the weight off his wrists, his hands turning purple from the strain.

Bruiser wheeled his horse around and charged at the man with the rope, swinging Asdelar's sword wildly. Two men jumped in his path, shouting and waving their arms. With another horse, this may have worked, but Bruiser was riding Asdelar's stallion, and the mounts of the Banam-hin were bred to be fearless. The bandits were run down, one man trampled and the other knocked aside with a shattered collarbone. The lasso-bearer stood dumbly, staring in surprise up until the moment Bruiser slashed his throat open.

The other horses weren't taking the ambush as well. They bucked and screamed, trying to retreat from the violence. In the commotion, one of the thieves ducked past the flying hooves and darted towards Asdelar, intent on capture.

Asdelar let him get within reach, then kicked high and hard, clipping the man right under the chin and knocking him out cold.

Bruiser's companions struggled to control their horses, cursing, but Roko and his one remaining man seemed to lose their nerve. Leaving the bodies in the street, they fled into a nearby alley.

"I'll cut out your liver next time I see you!" Bruiser roared at their backs. Sliding from his saddle, he reached out and grabbed the reins of one of the panicked horses, helping to keep the animal still.

"Cut me loose," Asdelar gasped, the pain in his hands and wrists almost too much to bear. "My hands—"

Bruiser ignored him until his companions were steady in their saddles once more. "You going to keep your legs to yourself?" he demanded, sending a significant look towards the unconscious bandit at Asdelar's feet. He swept the sword up to hover threateningly by Asdelar's face. "I'll cut you on my way down if you try anything stupid."

"Just cut these ropes! I can't walk or ride like this."

Grunting, Bruiser nodded to one of his men. "Do it and get him back up on that horse."

The man hesitated, looking at Asdelar with uneasy suspicion. Bruiser scowled at him impatiently. "He's not a Red. He's useless without his sword. And he knows," he sent Asdelar a significant glare, "that I'll cut his damned legs off if he tries anything stupid. He only needs to be able to talk, not walk."

Asdelar ground his teeth in frustration, but forced himself to cooperate. *Technically, they're taking me where I want to go*, he tried to reassure himself. *I'm going to need to face this Count sooner or later and see what he's up to*. As he settled himself back in the saddle and winced through the process of his hands being re-tied, his eyes traveled unconsciously back the way they had come.

Surely Hinego was hot on their trail. He'd figure things out. He'd come help Asdelar pull his chestnuts out of the fire. These imbeciles would never expect it; they thought they'd killed a Red.

Guilt spiked again at the thought of Fikin, and he swallowed hard. If only he'd made it clearer from the beginning that he wasn't interested, Fikin would never have been in his room trying to sweet talk him out of his trousers, and he and Hinego wouldn't have been arguing. His stupid flirting had gotten an innocent man killed and ruined any goodwill between himself and the one man who could possibly save his ass. Even if Hinego did come after him, it would be more to find Valera than to help him. He couldn't be expected to risk Valera's safety just to save Asdelar.

He was alone now with his guilt and without a sword. He would have to figure out a way to get his hands on a weapon, squeeze the answers out of the Count, and keep himself from getting killed.

This, he thought unkindly, *is all that damned girl's fault.*

~~*

They reached Lehaim two days later. Though a small town, it was a welcome reprieve after the filth- and crime-ridden streets of Jorwa. Bruiser and his men earned wary looks from the townspeople, but none seemed surprised to see the mercenaries riding openly down their streets. The few soldiers they passed—wearing secondhand leather armor that could stand to be washed and repaired, Asdelar noted disdainfully—only looked the other way and ignored his piercing look. There would be no help from that quarter.

The Count's manor, practically large enough to be a small castle, stood apart from the town, surrounded by old stone walls. The guards who let them in barely paid any attention to Asdelar. Without his armor and sword, he was just a battered prisoner of no importance. Stable boys ran up to take the horses, admiring the big war horse with shining eyes. Asdelar was yanked from his saddle, a dagger held snug against his ribs despite his bound hands.

"Move," Bruiser grunted, giving him a shove up the path that led to the manor's main entrance.

Asdelar looked around in growing confusion as they went. In the orchard, white ribbons fluttered from where someone had tied them to the branches. From every window hung a white and gold banner. Many long trestle tables had been dragged out onto the lawn, and servants were busily arranging flowers and white tablecloths.

"What's the big celebration?" he asked without thinking.

"Shuddup," Bruiser grunted and gave him another hard push to get him indoors.

More white banners and bustling servants awaited. Everyone in the manor was clearly preparing for some great event.

A manservant intercepted them in the foyer, looking them all over with faint disdain before waving them forward. "His Grace will see you in the Blue Room." Nose in the air, he led the mercenaries and their prisoner down the main hall and up the stairs.

Having been in the King's castle many times, Asdelar was not impressed by his surroundings, though Bruiser and his men looked around with barely concealed awe and greed at the tapestries and decorative vases lining the walls.

The manservant brought them to a stout oak door and knocked twice before opening it and gesturing for them to enter. Asdelar was first in and took a moment to inspect his surroundings swiftly.

The aptly named Blue Room was a large den for meeting guests in comfort and privacy. There was a roaring fire in a fireplace almost big enough for a man to stand in, and plush blue furniture. Even the flower arrangements and the rug were blue. A man was seated in an oversized armchair, one leg thrown indolently across one of the armrests as he sipped wine from a goblet, a servant hovering just behind him with a pitcher held ready for refills. Another man, gray and stooped with age, was seated in the chair closest to the fire, wrapped in thick furs despite the warmth of the room. He barely spared the visitors a glance, and his eyes were unfocused.

The younger man noted his disinterest. "Where are your manners, Father? We have guests." Clearly not expecting a reply, he set the goblet on a low dark table and got to his feet. He was tall and lean, with a sharp face and a hawkish nose. His eyes were set too far apart, and when he smiled the expression was unpleasant. His clothes were made of cheap material, though someone had tried to make them look similar to the fashion of the noblemen of the city. A slim dagger with a jade-encrusted hilt hung from his belt in a pretty little black sheath.

He placed his fists on his narrow hips and looked Asdelar up and down with faint curiosity. "This is one of the ones who you say has been tracking you? Who are you? Speak up, I haven't got all day." He gestured towards the window, the outside view blocked by another white and gold banner. "In case you hadn't noticed the decor, I'm preparing for my wedding, and don't have much spare time." An oily smile crossed his face. "Ah, but here I am complaining of my father's rudeness, and I haven't even introduced myself. I am Rewen Gray, Count of Lehaim."

Asdelar held himself straight and proud, gazing at the Count with an expressionless face. He gave a very small bow, bending at the waist. "Asdelar Lorem of the Banam-hin, swordsmen of the King. With all due respect, Your Grace, I report to His Majesty, and it is unlawful to imprison one of the Gravemen without just cause."

"Without just cause?" Rewen repeated, adopting a look of mock surprise. "You have been hounding my men and were planning on trespassing on my land. You came here armed, your intentions ignoble."

"Trespassing? I go in the name of the King," Asdelar interrupted sharply. "His word supersedes yours, Your Grace. As for my intentions, I come seeking Lady Valera Stimad of Thurul, relative of the King. I wished to ask if you'd seen her. If you have nothing to hide, then why send your thugs to capture me and bring me here bound like a slave?"

"Assuming you are not lying, which is doubtful, I'll have you know the Lady Valera has not been this far south," Rewen murmured, still smiling. "I have never even met the snippy little thing."

"And yet you seem to know her character."

Rewen sent Bruiser a brief glance.

Bruiser clouted Asdelar across the temple with a meaty fist, sending him staggering. "Shuddup," he snarled. "Watch your mouth when you speak to 'is Grace. You're not on the King's land no more." He gestured to one of his men, and the bag of Asdelar's belongings was thrown to the ground.

The magnificent armor spilled out, reflecting the firelight. Rewen's eyes lit up, and he picked up the breastplate, tracing with a thin finger the delicate patterns carved across the surface.

"I've heard of how beautiful the armor of the Banam-hin is, though I've never seen it up close." He tossed it to the floor carelessly. "It was made more to impress the masses than protect its wearer in battle. Pretty, but useless."

"That's because we are the elite," Asdelar sneered. "We do not expect an enemy's blade to ever get past our defenses. We do not need the armor, which is more than I can say for your shoddily-dressed soldiers."

"You say 'we', but I think you are nothing more than a fraud and a thief." Rewen looked at Bruiser expectantly. "There would have been a sword."

Reluctantly, Bruiser unbuckled the blade from around his thickset waist and offered it to Rewen, who took it eagerly.

"Ahh," he breathed, drawing the slender blade and admiring it in the firelight. "Excellent craftsmanship. Perfect balance." He twisted his hand, twirling the long sword experimentally. "These resemble dueling swords. Best for piercing and disarming, not slashing. Quick and deadly in the hands of someone who knows how to use one. I have fenced a bit. This sword pleases me. Since you have wrongfully stolen it from an owner you've no doubt slain, I will take it."

"Stolen?" Asdelar blurted, outraged. Two of the mercenaries restrained him when he tried to move forward. "What are you up to? Where is the Lady Valera? Give me that sword and I'll show you how a member of the Banam-hin repays traitors to the throne!"

But Rewen was not even looking at him anymore. Putting his dagger aside, he buckled on the sword belt and strode over to a mirror on the wall to admire the effect. "Kill him. Sink the armor in the pond. I want no evidence that he was ever here." He gestured towards a small coin purse on the table. "Your payment is there. Take it and go."

Asdelar slammed his elbow into the stomach of one of the men holding him and kicked the other in the kneecap, earning an agonized screech. Bruiser yanked the cudgel from where it hung from a cord on his belt and brought it down smartly between Asdelar's shoulders. He fell to his knees with a grunt, vision swimming. Everything from his waist up felt numb and far away for several terrifying moments.

The door swung open suddenly and a soldier stepped inside, hauling along a young woman by her elbow. She was struggling feebly, but stopped the instant Rewen turned to face her. "What have we here?"

"Sorry for the intrusion, Your Grace," the soldier grumbled, jerking the girl forward a pace when she tried to back off. "I caught 'er at the door tryin' to listen in at the keyhole."

"How does she keep getting out of her room?" Rewen demanded testily. "Blasted girl!" He strode over and gripped her chin in his hand, jerking her face up so he could meet her frightened gaze. "Behave, my dear," he said, voice dripping with insincere concern. "I would hate to have to lock my blushing bride-to-be in the dungeons for her own well-being. My my, but you have the worst case of cold feet I've ever seen."

Asdelar was still seeing double, but the sight of the long red hair jogged his memory. His voice was slurred as he spoke, attempting weakly to rise. "Lady Val—"

Bruiser grabbed a fistful of his hair and punched him in the face.

Releasing the gold locks, Bruiser let the unconscious man slump to the floor. "We'll take care of this fool," he promised, then sent the girl a sinister grin as he hastily scooped up the purse. "Good to see you again, your ladyship."

She glared at him in fearful loathing, but said nothing. Her eyes widened in comprehension as she saw the armor Jaks was stuffing back into the bag. Ducking her head to hide her expression, she clenched her fists and bit her tongue to keep silent.

Rewen was watching her keenly, however. "Wait." He went and stood over Asdelar's limp form, scratching his nose thoughtfully. "You said there was a Red with him?"

Bruiser nodded. "We killed 'im, though. He wasn't so tough."

"But how do we know there aren't more of them? I've never heard of a lone Blade so far from the King's castle, or a Red without a squad for that matter."

"We didn't see anybody else," Jaks said.

"Still ..." Rewen frowned. "I think I'd rather be safe than sorry. Leave him. Send in some men on your way out."

Bruiser gave an awkward half-bow and hustled his men out of the room.

"He can stew in the pit for a while," Rewen decided, smiling nastily. "After a few days without water and a few helpful prods with a knife, I'm sure he'll be more reasonable." He looked to his father as if for approval, but the old man had nodded off.

Two guards arrived in the doorway, standing stiffly to attention. "You wanted to see us, Your Grace?"

"Take this piece of trash downstairs and toss him in the pit. He's to have no food or water until I say so."

Valera bit the tip of her tongue to prevent herself from crying out. Rewen's temper was unpredictable, and she had the bruises to prove it. Begging for the Blade's life would probably do more harm than good. Tears swam in her eyes as her only hope at rescue was dragged from the room.

"Take her back to her room," Rewen commanded, shoving her towards the first guard and turning his back dismissively. He admired himself in the mirror once more, hand on the hilt of his new sword. "Make sure she stays there this time, or I'll hold you personally responsible."

The guard swallowed nervously and obeyed.

Valera was not the only one who had been witness to Rewen Gray's fits of violent temper.

Chapter Twelve

Hinego rode his mare as hard as he dared to make up for lost time, but he was still a day or two behind the kidnappers. He knew in his head that the chances of Asdelar still being alive and well were slim to none, but what other choice did he have but to follow? If he was lucky, the murderers would lead Hinego straight to Valera. As for Asdelar's fate, it was unfortunate, but he'd known the risks when he'd accepted the King's request.

Logically Hinego understood this, but he still let himself dwell as little as possible on Asdelar's well-being. If he was honest with himself, the thought of Asdelar's death bothered him more than he liked, and not just because he felt somewhat responsible. If he hadn't gone off in a huff to sulk and ask questions around town, Asdelar wouldn't have gotten caught in the first place.

The idiot was a tongue-wagging, naive pain in the ass, but Hinego would have given anything to take back the sharp words they had exchanged on the street. They had parted on bad terms, and Hinego had a sinking feeling he would never be able to make up for it. There was no reason for the murderers or their employer to keep Asdelar alive, especially if the man refused to talk. The Imalt-wor were trained to withstand vigorous torture and questioning, and he could only assume the Banam-hin had similar training.

All Asdelar had to look forward to was torture and death, thinking he'd failed his King, made an enemy of Hinego, and gotten Fikin killed.

Hinego was not used to feeling such intense guilt, and it ate him alive for the two days it took him to reach Jorwa.

He had never been to Jorwa, but he'd heard enough about it to know better than to march in wagging his authority in anyone's face. Without a squad to back him up, advertising himself as a sole Imalt-wor in such a lawless place was just asking to be killed, so he stripped off his telltale red sash stuffed it in his bag before entering the town limits. He'd have preferred to go around the town completely and forgo dealing with the criminals who made it their home, but it would take too long and there was always a chance that either Valera or Asdelar was being held by a criminal hoping to ransom them for easy money. A bit of coin was said to go a long way in Jorwa. So long as he asked the right people, he should be able to determine the fate of the two captives.

Completely ignoring the many sideways looks he earned—some suspicious, others calculating how much coin he had in his pockets—Hinego rode into the seedy town with his head high and his hackles raised.

He was in Jorwa mere minutes before someone decided to accost him.

Half a dozen men darted out of an alley, seizing his horse and penning him in with rusted blades and makeshift clubs.

"Are we the first?" one of them demanded.

Hinego frowned down at him, seemingly undisturbed by the obvious threat all around him. "First what?"

"You know. To stop you."

"Unfortunately for you, yes."

"Good, he's still got 'is money. Get 'im down."

Hinego slid from his saddle before anyone could reach for him and stood glaring at his attackers. "I suppose this is one way to get information. I'm looking for—"

"Shut your gods damned mouth," the leader spat, grabbing a fistful of Hinego's shirt and giving him a rough shake. "You say one more word—"

Hinego took the man's wrist and twisted hard. The man cried out sharply in pain, falling helplessly to his knees when the limb was turned even more brutally, threatening to break. "Stop stop stop! Leggo! Someone get 'im off!"

"Let go!" one of his cohorts commanded, stepping forward quickly to place his blade close to Hinego's throat.

Without releasing the hand in his grip, Hinego jerked to the side, out of reach, and felled the man with a stunning blow to the side of his head. The thief's eyes rolled up in his head and he fell bonelessly into the dirt.

Ignoring him, Hinego returned his attention to his captive. The other men shuffled back a step or two, uncertain what to do. "I said, I'm looking for someone. Not long ago, the other day maybe, a group of men came this way with a tall yellow-haired man. He might have looked a bit like nobility."

"Bruiser," the thug gasped, contorting his body oddly in an attempt to take some of the pressure off his trapped wrist. "Yeah, I saw 'im. It was Bruiser. He had the guy. Said he was takin' him to the Count. In Lehaim."

"Good." He rapped the man quickly between the eyes and let the unconscious thug fall over heavily. "Get out of my way," he said impatiently, and the other men fell back even further, visibly cowed.

Ignoring them, Hinego pulled himself back into his saddle and rode regally off.

~~*

Getting into the Count's manor was easy with his red sash back on display. Hinego was used to gaining swift acknowledgment from those in authority; refusing to see a Red was practically an admission of guilt. The guards, however, seemed even more uptight than they should have been by his arrival. While he stood in the foyer, left there by a soft-spoken servant who went to fetch the Count, Hinego watched the house guards out of the corner of his eye, suspicions roused. They were eyeing him warily and exchanging knowing looks. *He's gonna get it now*, those looks clearly said. Whether they meant the Count or Hinego, however, was up for debate. For the umpteenth time since arriving in the Count's lands, Hinego wished he'd waited for Imalt-wor backup.

The servant reappeared in the wake of a tall man tugging on riding gloves.

The imperious stare he turned Hinego's way gave away his identity before he even opened his mouth. "Yes, what is it?" the Count snapped. "I have a new horse to break in."

Hinego could be polite when he absolutely had to

be, but the young man's manner made him seethe inwardly. He inclined his head dutifully in greeting. "My name is Idra. I have a few questions for you, Your Grace, regarding Lady Valera Stimad. She's gone missing—"

Count Gray cut him off. "Stimad's lands are far north of here. What has this to do with me?"

Hinego stamped down on his temper as it flared up. "There's been strong evidence that she was headed south, possibly against her will. Your father is an old friend of the King. If she's simply running away, there's always a chance she would look here for a friendly face. Do you know if she came this way?"

"I doubt a young girl would be stupid enough to come all this way. She'd have to pass through Jorwa, and that cesspit would eat her alive." Gray tapped a riding crop against his leg as he spoke. "No girl has shown up *here*, anyway."

Hinego's eyes flickered towards the servant, still hovering in the background. The man was staring intently at the floor. He'd flinched just the tiniest bit at the Count's words.

"I see. Well, it was a long shot." Hinego raised a hand as if just remembering something. "Also, my companion was captured, and I've tracked his kidnappers to your lands. He is a member of the Banam-hin. Have you heard anything of this?"

"A Banam-hin so far from the castle? That's very unusual," Gray tutted, fussing with his gloves to avoid Hinego's gaze. "Jorwa is full of criminals and kidnappers. I would check there. I haven't heard anything of such a capture myself. I avoid the place as much as I can."

Which is why the crime there has gotten so out of

control, you lazy bastard, Hinego thought angrily, but kept his face passive. "Thank you for your help." He gestured to the white banners hanging from the walls. "I couldn't help but notice the decorations. Are you getting married? Who's the lucky lady?"

"The decorations are to please my addle-brained father. They have no significance." Gray eyed him shrewdly. "Where is your squad, Idra? I don't recognize you. I was under the impression the squad that was stationed here had already moved on."

"We are merely passing through. My men are waiting for me in Jorwa."

The Count didn't look like he'd bought it, but he let the matter drop. "Well, I am sorry I couldn't be of more help, but I haven't seen either of the people you're searching for. Now if that's all ..."

"Yes. Thank you. I'll show myself out." Hinego turned on his heel and left quickly.

As soon as he was gone, Rewen Gray turned on his servant, face red with anger. "Send someone to fetch that imbecile Bruiser," he said from behind clenched teeth. "This Red they claim to have taken care of is looking remarkably spry for a dead man."

~~*

Hinego lifted his eyes towards the moon, gauging how much longer he could afford to wait. He shifted his weight—carefully, so as not to draw any attention to himself—and pressed his back a little more firmly to the tree sheltering him in its deep shadows. His attention returned to the guards on the wall of the

Count's manor. He had their patrols memorized, but he would not risk moving just yet. It was close to midnight, and there was sure to be a shift change soon.

Valera was inside, he would have bet money on it. If he was going to act on his suspicions, it would have to be tonight. The Count was likely suspicious and jumpy due to his visit earlier in the day, and Hinego wasn't willing to give him time to do something drastic.

Like marry the King's great-niece.

Rewen's gall made Hinego clench his teeth. It had taken only a few pointed questions and coins to hear the juiciest rumor circulating Lehaim. Word was that the bachelor Count had found himself a bride, though he had thus far managed to keep her from the public eye. The white decorations in the manor combined with Gray's obvious distaste for his own territories made his intentions perfectly clear.

A marriage to one of the King's family members would make him more powerful, garner him better lands, and make him practically immune to backlash even from the King himself. Noble marriages were taken very seriously in Predala, especially when it came to royal blood. The King would be spitting hot coals, but he would be unwilling to make Valera a widow. Hinego's duty was clear: he must find Valera and get her out of Rewen Gray's reach as soon as possible. Asdelar's well-being was secondary. Even Asdelar would say as much.

Still, if he was lucky, perhaps Hinego would find him while searching for Valera. Assuming ...

His mind shied away from the idea, but the thought was already completing itself with cold finality: assuming the Count hadn't just had Asdelar killed on sight. He had most likely had Hinego's death in mind as well. A pair of men had been following him around Lehaim most of the afternoon, trying and failing to look casual about it. Giving them the slip had been pathetically easy, but it was just one more thing to make his need for action all the more urgent. He had to get to Valera tonight. Tomorrow might be too late for all of them.

He went tense as a new voice spoke up from the top of the wall overhead. The guards were being relieved. Now was his chance, while they were distracted.

He had tied his sash loosely around his neck, and tugged it up now to conceal the bottom half of his face. Crouching quickly to rub his hands in the dirt, he ran for the wall, keeping low and making as little noise as possible. He followed the curve of the wall around to the east side, just out of sight of the men at the front. He had circled the walls earlier in the evening before the light got too dim, avoiding the guards and doing a quick check of the mortar. The wall was old and parts of it were in ill repair. This particular section was cracked and crumbling. It was perfect for his needs.

Hand over hand he climbed his way to the top, jamming his fingertips and toes into crevices and praying he wouldn't put too much weight on a section unable to hold his weight. The wall was not very high, thank the gods, and he made it to the top in minutes, his fingers numb from the rough stone and his shoulders complaining mightily. Ignoring the aches and pains, he slipped down the first staircase he found and was in the courtyard in no time.

He paused to get his bearings. He wasn't sure where to find Valera, but the dungeons would be as good a place to start as any. As an added bonus, he was much less likely to run into any servants who might sound the alarm.

Liar, a little voice in his mind hissed, and he winced, ashamed and angry at himself.

Gray would not keep Valera in a dungeon. She was nobility. She would be locked up, but she would at least be a comfortable prisoner. If he was going to find anyone in the dungeons, it would be Asdelar. If he was even still alive. And right now Valera was Hinego's primary concern.

He waited until a cloud covered the moon and sprinted across the grounds. Security was fairly lax once he was away from the wall. There were sure to be guards inside, however. Hinego crept around the building, searching for the kitchen's back door. He had been trained to infiltrate, but it had been a long time since he'd actually put such skills to use. If he was caught, he would be killed, and there would be no one to help Valera. His heart was hammering in his ears, and he tensed at every small noise in the dark, but at last he found the door.

As with most estates, the kitchen's back door was a servants' entrance, a way for the help to go about their business without offending the eyes of the nobility. The chances of there being any guards in the vicinity were also slim to none. If he was lucky, a servant might have even carelessly left it unlocked.

He wasn't that lucky, but the lock was not complex. He swore softly as he worked at the lock with rusted pins, but was at last rewarded with a reluctant click.

Easing the door open just enough to permit him, he slipped inside.

He leaned against the door and forced himself to take several deep, steadying breaths. Now came the hard part. Parts of the manor were sure to be lit, and at any moment he could turn a corner and walk right into a guard or servant. There would be few places to hide, and he wasn't even sure where to begin his search.

Pushing himself away from the door, Hinego hurried through the large kitchen, careful to avoid the skillets and spoons hanging from the ceiling, and ducked into one of the servants' passageways. It was dark and narrow, and he kept one hand on the wall, his steps quick but light. The passage led to the main hall, and he hesitated, looking around carefully.

There was a single guard near the front door, but he was leaning heavily against a window picking at his nails with a dagger, his back to Hinego. Holding his breath and walking on the balls of his feet, Hinego crept across the hall towards the stairs. The bedrooms would be up there and were the most likely place where Valera would be.

A floorboard creaked overhead, and he froze. Someone was up. A pair of sleepy muffled voices came from somewhere near the top of the stairs, then began to descend. Hinego stood frozen, heart thudding, caught between the men on the stairs and the guard at the door.

Chapter Thirteen

Hinego looked around desperately for an escape route. He could probably make it back to the passageway on time, but if the men on the stairs were servants heading for that very passage, they'd discover him. Making a run for the dining room would put him in the guard's line of sight.

There was a door in the wall just past the staircase that he could make it to if he was quick, but if it was locked, he was as good as caught.

No choice.

As quickly and quietly as he could he dashed past the stairs to the door and tried the handle. It turned in his hand and he let out a sigh of relief, not stopping to think that there might be someone on the other side. Without a backwards look he opened the door and jumped inside, pulling the door shut quietly behind him.

He nearly tumbled down a flight of steep stone steps, caught off guard, and had to clutch the doorknob for balance. He peered warily down into the inky darkness. There was a torch on the wall, but it was obviously meant to be carried down; there were no other lights that he could see further down. After a moment's hesitation he began his descent, one hand gripping the sole wooden banister, the other held protectively out front to keep from running into a wall.

The winding stairs seemed to go on forever, and he was beginning to think he should turn around and take his chances with the guard upstairs when the wall curved inward suddenly, and he caught sight of a light around the corner. Pressing himself to the wall, he went down another three steps, straining his neck to see around the corner without exposing himself.

He'd found the dungeons.

There were two guards at a low wooden table, bleary eyes intent on the cards in their hands. Along the walls were chains and tools of torture, and there were old stains on the table and floor. Blood stains.

Hinego felt his lips peeling back from his teeth in disgusted horror. Torture was something reserved for only the most dangerous of criminals: traitors to the crown, spies, or slavers whose secrets had to be extracted as quickly as possible in order to save lives. The amount of blood and equipment here, however, suggested more use than someone in a backwater place like Lehaim should ever feel justified with. The Count, it seemed, was as depraved and violent as the very town at his borders that he showed such disdain for.

Hinego pulled his head out of sight and began to flex his arms and legs, mentally readying himself. He would have to do this quickly.

The guards had no warning.

Hinego flew out of the passage without a sound and was almost on them before the first of them managed to get to his feet with a cry of surprise. His hand barely made it to the sword at his belt before a fist slammed into his throat. He stumbled back and fell, clawing at his chest as he tried desperately to breathe.

The second guard actually had the presence of mind to leap out of the way, his sword out in his hands in a moment. He hesitated in shock for a vital moment, however, when his unarmed attacker came right at him. He took a hasty chop with his sword, but Hinego evaded the blow with liquid grace and slammed his knee right between the bigger man's legs.

The guard let out a high-pitched howl and doubled over, sword falling from nerveless fingers. Hinego hit him in the temple with his elbow as hard as he could, and the man collapsed limply, dead or very close to it.

Snatching up the fallen sword, Hinego turned to the other guard and slew him with a single vicious jab between the ribs. Still fighting for air, the man couldn't even let loose a scream.

Tossing the sword aside, Hinego bent over and relieved the dying man of the keys at his belt. Taking the lantern from the table, Hinego hurried to the far side of the dungeon. There were only half a dozen cells, and he went to each one in turn, holding his light up high and straining to make out a shape in the deep shadows. The smell was foul, but he blocked it out. Only two cells were occupied: one by a corpse, the other by a man gibbering quietly to himself who shrank away from the lantern light with a pitiful screech.

No Asdelar. No Valera.

Hinego cursed floridly. Valera must be upstairs after all. And Asdelar ...

He shut his eyes briefly, not prepared for the way his stomach clenched like a fist. It was his fault. If he'd gotten here sooner ... If he'd not had that ridiculous tiff with Asdelar back in Belor, he would have been able to easily take down the men who had accosted Asdelar and Fikin. Instead Count Gray had killed Asdelar in an attempt to cover his tracks.

The Count was going to pay for this. For all of this.

He was turning away, teeth clenching and unclenching in wordless rage and regret, when he noticed the grate in the floor.

He'd passed it without a second look after he'd finished off the guards, assuming it was drainage for when the blood and piss and refuse was washed off the walls and floors. But the grate was far too large; more than big enough for a man. As he approached it, the smell coming from within hit him like a physical blow. He gagged and paused to tighten the sash around his face. Setting the lantern aside, he seized the grate and dragged it to one side with a grunt of effort.

It was a pit. He'd heard of such things before: places for prisoners to be thrown and forgotten. It was an effective way of breaking a man, forcing him to wallow in his own filth with no light or food for however long it took. Sooner or later he'd be begging for the chance to talk in return for sweet sunlight and air.

Holding his breath in anticipation as much as to block out the stench, Hinego lay on his belly at the edge of the yawning hole and lowered the lantern as far as he could reach. The pit was too deep for the light to reach the bottom, and too high for a man to jump or climb out, though the slick muddy walls would have made that impossible regardless.

"Asdelar?"

There was no response, and after a long tense moment Hinego felt dread begin to rise up in him again. No one was there. Or ... what if there was only a *body?*

Then something below rustled or squelched—something *moved.* "Hinego?" the voice was raspy and bone-tired, but unmistakable.

Hinego's mouth stretched in a quick grin before he caught himself. "You're a lost cause, Blade. I turn my back on you for a matter of hours and you try your damnedest to get yourself killed."

The replying laughter was weak but welcome. "I live to make your life difficult. I don't suppose we could continue this argument somewhere less hellish?"

"Wait." Setting the lantern aside, Hinego got to his feet and cast about for rope. He settled for a length of chain. "Are you strong enough to climb up? I won't be able to pull your dead weight unassisted."

Asdelar's voice was heavy with exhaustion. "I think so. I can try. I tried to let them think they broke me early, to save some of my strength." His hollow laugh echoed up from the pit again. "Hope it's enough."

Hinego tossed one end of the chain down and wound the other end around the arm where Dora's gauntlet protected him. "Come on. We don't have much time."

It took a while, with Hinego barely managing to support his weight and Asdelar being forced to stop once or twice to catch his breath, but at last his head appeared over the edge of the pit. He got one elbow up, then two, and Hinego dropped the chain to seize the man under the armpits and haul him bodily up and out.

Exhausted by their efforts, they collapsed on the ground, panting.

Asdelar rolled painfully onto his stomach, putting his face right against the floor. "Oh, thank the gods," he breathed. "I felt like I was down there forever. I thought I was going to die in there."

Hinego was staring at his bare back and the ugly welts and cuts that covered him from shoulders to hips. Someone had gone at him with a whip or a cane. Rage bubbled inside of Hinego like acid.

When Asdelar finally lifted his head, his face was a mess of bruises and mud, and he looked as if he'd been a few steps closer to death than was good for him. His swollen lips made an attempt at a crooked smile. "Thank you," he said quietly.

Hinego shrugged, unable to meet his eyes, and rose to his feet slowly. "I'm here for Valera," he said without thinking. "I wasn't sure I'd even find you here. I thought ..."

"I figured he'd kill me," Asdelar agreed, and allowed Hinego to pull him to his feet. "But first he wanted to know if there would be anyone else coming. I told him there was an entire legion of Banam-hin hot on my trail, but I don't think he bought it. Still, I guess he thought it'd be useful to keep me alive a little longer. Just in case." He winced, touching his face with delicate fingers. "I look like someone hit me with a tree branch, don't I?"

"Repeatedly and with great enthusiasm," Hinego said dryly. "Your ridiculous Rover can play nursemaid when we get out of here. But first we have to find Valera."

"Fikin's alive?" Asdelar gave a groan of relief,

covering his face briefly with his hands. "I was so sure he was dead. There was so much blood ... They thought he was you."

"He should live," Hinego said brusquely. "What of Valera? Do you know if she's here?"

Asdelar lowered his hands and gave himself a shake, visibly trying to collect himself and push thoughts of his ordeal to the back of his mind. "She's here, all right. I saw her. Apparently she keeps managing to escape from her room, so she's going to be guarded. Poor kid's absolutely terrified. I think that lunatic Rewen plans to marry her."

Hinego nodded. "I had an audience with him earlier today. We need to get clear of here tonight before he does something stupid. Are you fit to fight at all?"

Asdelar went over to the dead guards and took one of the short swords, swinging it a few times to test the weight and balance. "I feel like I've been trampled by a horse, but nothing's broken, and they didn't hit me in the head *too* hard. I should be fine, but let's try to avoid fighting every guard in the place."

"Agreed. Any idea where her room is?"

"No, but I'm assuming the Count would keep her pretty close. My guess is the top floor." Asdelar stretched carefully, touched his toes, and gave the sword another determined swing. He drew in a deep breath. "If we're going to do this, let's do it before I collapse."

Hinego hesitated. "If you think you can slip outside unseen, you can wait for us there."

"Is that concern I detect?" Asdelar teased.

Hinego scowled, marching past. "You might slow

me down, that's all."

"I'll be fine, Hinego. Really. Besides, you could use a sword at your back. But ..." Asdelar had turned towards the cells and was frowning. "What about that man? We can't just leave him here."

"Put your bleeding heart away, Blade," Hinego snapped, one foot already on the stairs. "For all you know, the man deserves to be here. He could be a murderer."

"Or just another victim of the Count's cruelty," Asdelar argued. "Can't we just let him go?"

"So he can go running through the manor getting the attention of every guard in the place? No. We can't risk it. Besides, after we report Rewen, the King's going to send a lot more Gravemen here to deal with him. They can figure out what to do about any prisoners then."

Asdelar nodded reluctantly and followed him without further protest.

They stumbled up the dark staircase, haste replacing caution. They had no way of knowing when the prison guards would be relieved, and once the bodies were discovered a full-out manhunt would begin.

Once at the door, Hinego held up a hand and put his ear to the wood, listening intently. After a moment he opened the door a crack, then paused, waiting for a shout of alarm. Nothing. Nodding silently to Asdelar, he opened the door carefully and squeezed out. He took two steps into the main hall and froze. He didn't even have time to warn Asdelar, who had come out right on his heels.

The hall was filled with guards.

They stood still as statues, every one of them with

his sword drawn, staring belligerently at the intruders. For a long moment there was a tense silence as Hinego's mind raced. There were nearly a score of them, far too many for himself and Asdelar to take on, even if the he'd been in better shape. Hinego found himself instinctively shifting into a fighting stance anyway, and out of the corner of his eye saw Asdelar raise his sword.

None of the guards made any move to attack, however. Instead, the one with a Captain's stripe on his chest stepped to the side to let pass a man previously hidden from sight.

Hinego's breath hissed out from between clenched teeth.

Rewen Gray. In one hand he was holding Asdelar's sword. The other was clamped firmly around the thin arm of a petrified girl—Lady Valera. She stared at her would-be rescuers with wide-eyed panic, her face white and tear-streaked. Her eyes were puffy from crying and lack of sleep, and she kept cringing instinctively away from Rewen like a kicked dog.

The look on Rewen's face was triumphant. "Just how stupid do you think I am, *Red*?" he mocked. "I knew you'd try something. My men searched Jorwa; no Imalt-wor have been reported. You're on your own. I have to admit, while I suspected you'd consider breaking in tonight, I was half convinced you weren't suicidal enough to actually go through with it. Impressive that you got this far, but you'll get no further." His grip must have tightened on Valera's arm, because she gave a pained whimper. "Now, unless you want me to do something permanently disfiguring to this insipid girl, I suggest you give yourselves up quietly."

Hinego yanked the red sash down from his face furiously, his voice ringing out commandingly. "I am Hinego Idra, Imalt-wor of the King's Gravemen. You are guilty of treason, Count Gray, and all you men who stand with him will suffer the same punishment. I am acting on behalf of the King and that overrules your Count's authority."

Asdelar stepped up beside him, his tone colder than Hinego had ever heard it and full of an unexpected authority. "Asdelar Lorem, Banam-hin. You have kidnapped and restrained a relative of the King and imprisoned a Graveman without just cause. These crimes are punishable by death. Release the Lady Valera immediately and perhaps the King will show mercy."

Several of the guards exchanged nervous looks.

Rewen threw back his head and laughed. "Is this a joke? You're not in the castle anymore, boy. You have no power here. You idiots came here all alone. No one ever has to know you were even here."

"You place a great deal of trust in your men," Hinego said. "Do you really think you can convince every soldier here to keep this to himself?" He glared around at the guards. "Do you know what will happen when the King inevitably finds out what happened here? For your silence, you'll be hanged. There may be no Gravemen in the area, but don't think me a complete fool, Count. In a few days a squad of Imalt-wor will be here to ask very pointed questions. They know of my suspicions, and they know I was headed here. If they don't find me, it's going to go very badly for you."

The guards began to mutter amongst themselves.

"He's bluffing," Rewen snarled, glaring at Hinego.

"If there was any backup to be found, he'd have come here with it. These two were the only ones sent on the search." He turned on the Captain. "Kill them both. Dispose of the bodies. That's an order."

The Captain hesitated for just an instant. Before he could decide one way or the other, Asdelar suddenly took two quick strides forward, raising the sword up to place his lips to the hilt in a brief challenge. "Count Rewen Gray, I challenge you!"

Everyone went still.

Hinego's heart felt like it had jumped up into his throat.

Rewen gaped at Asdelar for a long moment. Abruptly his lips curled up in an artful sneer. "You can't be serious."

Asdelar's eyes were like ice. "If you are too much of a yellow-bellied coward to agree to an honest duel with a wounded man, you do not deserve the right to even look upon these men, much less command them. I challenge you, Your Grace. If I win, we walk free, along with the Lady Valera. Do you accept?"

The guards were all looking at their Count expectantly. Rewen's face flushed slowly with anger. He shoved Valera aside, and the Captain caught her clumsily.

"I accept," Rewen growled. "After I've cut out your kidneys and fed them to my dogs, die knowing that your friend will be taking your place in the pit to die slowly." He turned and barked orders for a soldier to bring him his dueling gauntlets.

Hinego seized Asdelar by the elbow and dragged him away a few feet, his voice a low hiss. "Lorem, are you *insane*? I thought you said they *didn't* hit you on the head."

"I said they didn't hit me *too hard*."

"This is no time for jokes!"

"Relax, Hinego. I can take this pompous prick." He paused. "I'm pretty sure, anyway."

"He'll kill you. He's got your sword, and you look like you can barely stand up."

"What other choice do we have? We can't fight them *all*. If they were going to turn on Rewen, they'd have done it already."

"You idiot," Hinego said, furious. The worst part was that he knew Asdelar was right. "Fine, a duel. But *I'll* do it."

"No, Hinego. You don't know how to use a sword, and he'll never agree to hand-to-hand with a Red. He knows he'd never beat you that way." Asdelar lowered his head to touch his forehead briefly to Hinego's, taking him off guard. "If he kills me, do me a favor and take out as many of these bastards as you can."

Hinego glared at him helplessly. "I owe you an apology for Belor," he said abruptly. "So if you want to hear it, don't die."

Asdelar gave a short, breathy laugh. "All right." His smile faded into a frown as the soldier came hurrying back with the thick leather gauntlets meant to help block incoming blows. "The man's a real piece of work. He's going to take every advantage he can get."

Hinego looked at Asdelar's bare arms and torso. He had nothing to protect him from the longer reach of the Count's stolen blade. He reached up and pulled the red sash from around his neck. "Give me your arms," he muttered, and hastily wrapped the cloth around one proffered forearm, trying not to knot it too tightly. Rolling up his own sleeve, he unbuckled Dora's gauntlet and transferred that to Asdelar's other arm. "It's better than nothing, anyway."

Asdelar looked touched. "Hey, in case this bastard really does run me through, I have to know ..."

"What, idiot Blade?" Hinego grumbled, staring at the makeshift arm guards rather than look him in the face.

"What you said ... that night when we were playing Truth or Fancy ... was that true?"

Hinego forced himself to lift his eyes. Asdelar's smile was teasing, but there was a nervousness to his gaze as well. Hinego offered a mock scowl. "You'll have to live to find that out as well."

Asdelar blinked, then smiled ruefully. "Stubborn." He turned to face the Count, hefting the sword once more, still trying to get used to the weight. "Ready yet, *Your Grace?*"

The soldiers had spread out, leaving plenty of space in the middle of the great hall for the duel. Reluctantly Hinego fell back as well, sticking close to the wall.

Rewen had just finished tightening the laces on his gauntlets to his liking and gave Asdelar's sword a fancy twirl. "I look forward to putting you out of your misery, *boy*. Let's finish this."

They came close together, and Asdelar bent at the waist in a quick bow. Rewen did not bother with such formalities. He lunged forward, driving the sword directly at Asdelar's chest. Hinego bit his tongue hard.

Asdelar managed to jerk back and avoid the blow, bringing his sword up in a swift counter that batted the more slender blade aside easily. The duel began in earnest, and it quickly became obvious that the odds were in the Count's favor.

He was clearly a skilled duelist, and his attacks were constant and relentless. His blade was also significantly longer than Asdelar's, making it easier for him to get past his guard. Asdelar was fighting with a sword much different from the one he was accustomed to; it was short and thick and heavy, meant more for slashing and chopping than anything else. He was wounded and exhausted from his ordeal in the dungeons, and clearly a bit unsteady on his feet. He stumbled twice, and wasn't able to deflect one particularly vicious swipe, earning him a dark red slash across his ribs.

Hinego began edging his way closer and closer to Valera. Everyone's attention was on the fight. If Asdelar were to lose, perhaps Hinego could catch the guards by surprise and snatch Valera away. One eye on the fight, he waited for his chance and prayed he wouldn't need to take it.

The two men danced across the room, steel ringing against steel, their faces taut with concentration. As Asdelar adjusted to the strange sword, however, a new fact became apparent. He was *good*. Even injured and with an unfamiliar blade, it quickly became obvious how he had earned his place with the Banam-hin. His feet moved more lightly, his swings gained more control, and if anything, he became faster. It wasn't long before the Count was forced to fall on the defensive, teeth bared in frustrated rage.

Hinego, who had only ever seen his companion wield a sword for a few brief encounters, was impressed. He found himself wondering just how dangerous and graceful Asdelar would be in a proper duel with his full strength. A quick glance around the room showed the guards were likewise spellbound. An expression of respect was stamped on the Captain's weathered face. Even Valera's eyes were wide with borderline adoration.

Still, if Asdelar was going to win, it would have to be soon, Hinego thought grimly. He was running on adrenaline, but soon he would be unable to go on. He needed rest and medical attention. All it would take would be one sign of weakness, and it would be but the work of a moment for Rewen to take him down with one well-aimed thrust.

As if he had somehow cursed the other man by his very thoughts, Asdelar suddenly seemed to falter. His parry was clumsy, and his blade sagged towards the floor as if he could no longer bear the weight of it. His shoulders hunched and he swayed backwards, visibly fighting for breath.

Rewen's mouth spread in a savage smile, and he dove forward, arm extended to its full length as he struck at the exposed throat.

Hinego heard someone yell—it sounded like his own voice. But Asdelar was already moving. It had been a feint.

He leaned backwards swiftly, avoiding the blade, and brought his sword up and around in a vicious arc. The Count's leather gauntlet took the brunt of the blow, but could not deflect it entirely. Momentarily numbed by the hit, his hand opened reflexively, and his sword clattered to the ground. Asdelar took a step forward into Rewen's guard, blade swishing forward once more, only to freeze a breath away from the startled Count's throat.

"I yield," Rewen gasped.

Valera gave an involuntary little shriek of joy, then clapped her free hand to her mouth hastily to stifle the sound.

Asdelar kicked aside the fallen sword, never taking his narrowed eyes from the Count's face. He was breathing harshly, muscles visibly quivering from the effort the fight had cost him.

"We are leaving," he said, loud enough for the guards to hear. Many of them had reached automatically for their weapons at their lord's defeat. "If you men are at all loyal to your King, you'll have this traitorous bastard thrown in his own dungeons until the Gravemen arrive."

"You can't just let him live," Valera cried, outraged. "He'll send his men after us the instant we're out of the manor! He'll run and hide from the law!"

Asdelar shook his head slightly, and Hinego swallowed a groan. Curse the man's bizarre code of honor. It was unbelievable that the same mercy that had preserved the lives of the thieves at the beginning of their journey now stayed his hand with a man who fully deserved the death hovering by his jugular.

The Captain gazed at Asdelar, face unreadable. Then slowly he relaxed his grip on Valera and released her. "Stand down," he commanded his guardsmen. Hinego watched them warily as they obeyed. There was no telling if the Captain was honoring Asdelar's victory or merely ensuring that no further harm came to the Count. He beckoned for Valera, and she hastily moved away from the guards and rushed to hide behind Hinego.

Emboldened by her new human shield, she raised

her voice to a servant Hinego hadn't noticed hovering in the kitchen passageway. "You! Boy! Fetch some rope." Startled by her commanding tone, the boy turned and fled. Valera frowned at Hinego. "I don't trust Gray. We can at least tie the bastard up."

Hinego grunted in agreement.

The servant returned promptly with a length of rope, and Hinego took it from him and crossed the hall. Valera stuck close, practically stepping on his heels.

Asdelar slowly lowered his blade, taking his eyes from the Count for an instant to flash Hinego a weary smile. "Told you I had everything under control."

Hinego rolled his eyes, stepping forward and snatching up one of the Count's hands. "Yes, we're all very impressed. Sit down before you fall—"

Rewen moved swiftly, taking advantage of the temporary distraction. He yanked his pretty jeweled dagger out of his boot and lunged at Hinego with it.

Hinego lurched back, arm snapping up defensively, and a hiss of surprised pain escaped from behind clenched teeth as the blade bit deep into his arm. Valera screamed. Then Asdelar was moving impossibly fast, his arm flashing out like a snake to sink his blade through the base of Rewen Gray's throat.

Blood splashed Hinego in the face, and he shut his eyes instinctively, his mouth full of a hot coppery tang.

The Count made a desperate gurgle and staggered back before falling heavily to the ground, fighting feebly to extricate the sword. Hinego was dimly aware of Valera huddling up against his back, her face pressed between his shoulder blades to hide from the sight.

Many of the guards cried out and moved forward, but the Captain gave a sharp command that froze them in their tracks.

Strong arms took Hinego by the shoulders and turned him around sharply. Asdelar's face was pale, his voice stricken. "*Hinego—?*"

"I'm fine," Hinego growled, unaccountably embarrassed by Asdelar's alarm. He winced slightly as he checked the nasty wound on his arm. The cut was deep, nearly to the bone. It was bleeding all over the place. Valera caught a glimpse of it over his shoulder and gave a low moan.

Asdelar yanked the red sash from his arm and began binding the wound tightly and efficiently. "The cowardly scum," he muttered fiercely. "I should have killed him during the duel."

Hinego shook his head. "It doesn't matter. He's no threat anymore." As his adrenaline slowly ebbed, he became aware of just how much the damned arm *hurt*, and struggled to block out the pain. He could not afford to show weakness until he knew the ultimate intentions of the guardsmen.

With a sigh of utter exhaustion, Asdelar bent and retrieved his stolen blade, giving the hilt a swift, almost affectionate kiss. Hinego, half expecting him to sit on the stairs and take a breather, stared in disbelief as the Banam-hin turned towards the tense guards and lifted his sword in yet another challenge.

"This man has been brought to justice for his deeds. Should any of you feel the unwise urge to avenge your lord, now is the time. But make it quick. We have places to be."

The men gaped at him, speechless. Then the

Captain stepped forward, looking suspiciously like he was biting back a smile. He drew his sword and saluted Asdelar with it respectfully, then set the weapon deliberately on the ground. "His lordship betrayed the crown with his actions, and broke the rules of an honorable duel. You'll find no quarrel with my men. We are loyal to the crown."

The rest of the guards quickly followed his example, placing their swords on the ground after a quick salute.

"Lord Gray's father must be informed, even if he is unable to understand what transpired." The Captain nodded to one of his men, who hurried upstairs. "We have a Red Cove here in Lehaim where you would perhaps feel safer. I will send the Count's personal doctor there and see about getting your horse returned to you, Sir Blade."

"Thank you, Captain," Asdelar said graciously.

The man nodded and selected half a dozen men. "Escort them to the Red Cove. Make sure they make it there safely."

Hinego almost refused the escort, then bit back his protests with an internal sigh. Asdelar wouldn't be able to stay on his feet much longer, and Hinego had already lost more blood than he liked. If one of them were to collapse on the path, the guards would be there to get them to their destination and make sure they weren't robbed blind by night bandits.

Asdelar went to stand by Hinego, watching as some of the guards came forward to take care of the Count's body. "I believe you said something about an apology," he murmured, his serious tone ruined by the smile twitching at his mouth.

Hinego ran a hand through his hair, suddenly

uncomfortable. "I apologize for the way I treated you and Fikin," he finally said, voice gruff. "I ... can be a jerk. I'm not sure if you noticed."

Asdelar gave a low laugh. "I had, actually. It's all right. I think I'm beginning to understand how your deranged little brain works." He sighed heavily, sheathing his sword. "I think I could really really use a drink after all of this."

"I think a doctor and a good night's rest are first on the agenda," Hinego pointed out dryly, and turned to Valera. "Are you all right, my lady?"

"Yes." She nodded, still pale but clearly beginning to regain her dignity. "Thank you. Both of you. My great-uncle sent good men. Rewen Gray would have used me as a political pawn, and you've done your King a great service as well as myself. I admit, I was worried when I realized it was just the two of you, but you faced nearly impossible odds and won."

"Hey, we're Gravemen," Asdelar said with a ghost of his old charming smile. "Doing the impossible is in the job description."

Chapter Fourteen

The Captain of the guard proved himself to be a more honorable man than his lord. Hinego, Asdelar, and Valera were sequestered safely in the Red Cove and tended to by a skilled doctor. In the days it took the three of them to sufficiently recover their strength, the Captain had the manor's wedding decorations torn down, the Count buried, and a formal apology and explanation penned.

Valera promised to be sure it fell into the King's hands, along with a good word for the Captain's sake to ensure he and his men were shown mercy. They had not treated her badly during her stay at the manor, and as the terror of her ordeal faded, she became more imperious and demanding every day. Asdelar humored her, clearly used to dealing with spoiled nobles, but Hinego began looking for excuses to stay away from the inn.

On the fifth day, Morasa and her squad marched into Lehaim, clearly looking to do battle. She was surprised and relieved to find them safe and sound at the Cove.

"We headed here as soon as we got your message from that silly bird of yours," she explained as they all took lunch together on the main floor. "I had a bad feeling that slimy bastard Rewen couldn't be trusted. Looks like I was right, though you seem to have handled yourselves just fine without us." She gave a cluck of concern, eyeing the bandages wrapped around Hinego's forearm. "Looks like you managed to walk into someone's sword, though, you clumsy oaf."

"You should see the other guy," Hinego muttered into his bread.

Morasa gave a bark of sharp, startled laughter. "Well I'll be damned. I knew you had a sense of humor hidden somewhere. Maybe you should go on these sorts of adventures more often. Or perhaps it's just the company you keep." She sent Asdelar a smile and a wink.

Asdelar barely showed signs of the torture he'd undergone—at least to the casual eye. It was likely he would always bear the scars on his back, and every time Hinego caught a glimpse of them when they were dressing in the mornings, he felt a hot anger deep in his stomach.

Asdelar smiled back sunnily at Morasa and changed the subject. "Personally I can't wait to see the last of this place. I hope you don't feel like sightseeing, because we're ready to get on the road any time you are."

She nodded. "We can leave in the morning if you like."

Valera had been silent throughout the meal, obviously unused to eating with "the help" but still unwilling to be left alone. "I can't wait to go home," she blurted, then ducked her head.

"Your parents must be going through hell right now," Asdelar pointed out. "Our message of your rescue won't reach them for another few days. I hope you know better than to put them through this again by pulling another of your silly running away stunts."

Hinego drew in a quick breath. Though her face

reddened in a flash of humiliated anger, Valera did not lose her temper. She had come to view Asdelar as her own personal white knight.

"I won't," she said with only a hint of petulance.

"Good girl," Morasa said brightly, making Hinego tense up again. "Now, what say you and I do a little shopping?"

Valera stared at her, as nonplussed by the offer as she was by the easy familiarity. "Shopping?"

"Well, yes. I'm sure you're tired of wearing the same dress every day. It's gotten pretty ragged with everything you've been through." At the time of her rescue Valera had been wearing a dress provided to her by the Count, but she had changed into the outfit she'd been kidnapped in the moment she got the opportunity. She had no wish to keep anything given to her by the man she despised so much. "I doubt we'll be able to find anything here to suit your standards, but it will be better than nothing, right?"

Valera nodded hesitantly. "All ... all right."

"Splendid." Morasa addressed her squad. "Elaine, Bonun, you'll come with us. Irgan, Resh, Julian, you're on supply duty. Hop to it. Let's leave these two to some peace and quiet." As she got to her feet, she sent Hinego a pointed look that confused him completely.

The Imalt-wor rose to their feet, scraping back their chairs and stuffing the last of the food in their mouths. They followed their leader from the inn, Valera trailing in their wake.

Asdelar cleared his throat and set his tankard aside after they'd left. "If you're finished, I'd like to check that." He nodded at Hinego's bandaged arm.

Hinego grunted in compliance and allowed the

other man to lead the way upstairs to the room the three of them had been sharing. Valera had been given her own room, but had refused to use it. Despite the reappearance of her famed superior manner, she was still terrified of being left alone. Not even Hinego had the heart to refuse her. She'd been sleeping in his bed, while he'd taken to sleeping on a blanket just by the door.

Hinego had pulled Asdelar aside to have a firm talk with him on the first night. "Be gentle around her, and none of your 'harmless' flirting. For weeks now she's been in the company of men who ... might have made her captivity all the more unbearable."

Asdelar had tugged playfully on a lock of Hinego's hair, grinning at the impatient look it earned him. "Your tact is sweet, but I don't think you have to worry about her. I'm willing to bet a lot of coin that Valera's father gave her a chastity belt for her sixteenth birthday." He'd laughed loudly at the furious blush that stained Hinego's face and there was no more uneasiness about allowing Valera to camp out in their room.

Hinego seated himself on the edge of his bed, and Asdelar took a seat beside him. He began unwrapping the bandages, constantly checking Hinego's face for any indication of discomfort. Changing the bindings had been painful for the first two days, as the threads tended to stick to the clotting blood.

Asdelar wadded up the bandage and tossed it into a corner, inspecting the stitched wound judiciously. "No pus, no more bleeding, and it doesn't look red or puffy. I think it's going to heal nicely."

Hinego lifted a brow. "Miss your calling as a doctor, Lorem?"

Asdelar laughed briefly, dabbing at the arm with a damp rag to clean it. "I'm a sword fighter, Hinego. I've seen my share of wounds. The medics for the Banamhin are always busy tending to clumsy apprentice Blades." He selected a clean strip of cloth from the material the doctor had provided and wrapped the wound carefully. After he was finished, his fingertips lingered on Hinego's arm, his head lowered and face hidden behind his hair.

"A part of me keeps thinking I shouldn't have killed him," he said softly. "The Count. I could have hit him in the head instead. Hell, if I'd just waited a few more seconds, I'm sure *you* would have disarmed him easily. I just ... I thought he was going to kill you. I couldn't stand that. I didn't stop to think." He gave a slightly shaky sigh. "I knew I couldn't wield a blade and not kill someone someday. I guess I just always assumed it would happen in a great battle, and I wouldn't have time to process it. This was ... up close and personal. He was just a stupid, arrogant man, and I killed him when I should have left him for the King's justice."

"Well, personally I'm glad you *did* kill the little prick," Hinego said with a wry smile.

Asdelar laughed quietly. "At least all of this mess is over with. And Morasa said Fikin looked alive and well when she passed through Belor ..."

Hinego pulled his arm free. "He'll be happy to see you again," he said, voice neutral. "The idiot begged me to take him with me."

Asdelar shook his head, mouth twitching in a smile. "He's a good friend, even if he can't take a hint."

It's none of your business, Hinego's brain insisted,

but he heard himself ask, "What hint?"

"He, ah ..." Asdelar looked away as if embarrassed, plucking at a loose thread in the thin blanket. "He made a pass at me right before we were attacked in Belor. I turned him down, but he seems like the persistent type."

"You turned him down?" Hinego repeated, and winced at the incredulity he heard in his own tone.

Asdelar had heard it, too. He glared at Hinego. "Why is it that you've assumed that I'm a sex addict since the minute we met? I've had my fair share of lovers, yes, but what business of it is yours, anyway? It's not like I made any of them any promises or did anything unsafe. I'm an adult, I can do what I like. That doesn't mean I'll fall into bed with everyone who bats their lashes at me."

Hinego held up his hands to stem the angry tirade, feeling himself flush in unexpected shame. "I know," he interrupted. "I mean, I know it's ... none of my business. I didn't—I just—" He ran a hand through his hair and sighed in frustration.

It was his turn to avert his gaze. He was silent for a long moment, and when he spoke, his voice was quiet and grudging. "My last lover was promiscuous. Even while we were in a relationship, monogamy was apparently a foreign concept. I put up with it for almost two years before Morasa finally convinced me to walk out. It's ... left me a little bitter. And judgmental. I ... apologize. It doesn't help that I've never been good at dealing with people. You already annoyed me and I took your flirtatious manner a little too personally."

The anger was gone from Asdelar's face. "Apology accepted," he said graciously. "I think I can understand that. Though I wish you'd told me earlier." He grinned suddenly. "And don't think I missed that distinct lack of pronouns. You said if I lived through that duel you'd tell me the truth."

"What are you talking about?" Hinego asked, feigning ignorance.

Asdelar looked dismayed. "What am I—? You grumpy-faced tease, you said you'd never been with a man and I want to know the truth, gods damn—" His voice petered off abruptly as calloused fingers slid up along his jaw, past his ear, and buried themselves in his hair. His breath frozen in his lungs, he stared at Hinego's face from inches away.

"I lied," Hinego said solemnly. "Are you happy now, you infuriating Blade?"

Asdelar's grin was giddy and playful all at once. "You have no idea," he murmured. Then Hinego's warm mouth was on his, and there was no more talking for a long time after.

Fin

About the Author

When she's not working on fifty thousand half-finished stories at once, Melissa is usually playing an obscene amount of video games or doodling goofy comics. She lives in North Carolina with her sister and her extremely spoiled cat, and has nowhere near enough room to stash all her books.

She has a weakness for writing and reading fantasy, as real life is depressing and disappointing enough half the time. She also has a penchant for writing about in-denial and emotionally stunted romance interests, and lives for long drawn-out UST and relationship development.

...Though she's secretly a bit of a prude. (Don't tell anyone.)

She can be found at http://homicidalmuse.blogspot.com/ and on twitter @homicidalmuse.

CPSIA information can be obtained at www.ICGtesting.com
Printed in the USA
LVOW132024160613

338791LV00001B/24/P